REPENTANCE OF THE SOUTHERN BURDEN

REPENTANCE OF THE SOUTHERN BURDEN

BY: J.R.GRAY-HEIM

Published by Josadah Publishing Co.

Josadah Publishing Co., 169 Bridle Drive, Raeford, NC 28376, U.S.A.

Repentance of the Southern Burden
Copyright © 2021 by J.R. Gray-Heim.

All rights reserved. Printed in the United States of America. No part of this book may be used or reproduced in any manner whatsoever without written permission except in the case of brief quotations embodied in critical articles or reviews.

This book is a work of fiction. Names, characters, businesses, organizations, places, events and incidents either are the product of the author's imagination or are used fictitiously. Any resemblance to actual persons, living or dead, events, or locales is entirely coincidental.

www.jrgrayheim.com

Cover design by Raul Rubiera

Hardcover ISBN: 978-1-7373626-1-6
Paperback ISBN: 978-1-7373626-0-9

This is a Josadah Publishing Co. Book.

Dedication

For My Husband, Adam

Whose companionship, warmth, and love helped nurture my creative side. And without him, my dreams would never be possible.

For My Dear Friend Teresa

Even though she gained her wings before the completion of this book, her unconditional love and friendship catapulted this book from a simple idea to actual reality. Her earthly presence will be forever missed.

Author's Note

Dear Reader,

This book deals with the delicate topics of sexual discovery, exploration and sexual acts; which can be hard for some people to read.

In this book, I describe the realities of the affects of childhood trauma, family issues and very real depictions of sexual thoughts and acts. This book uses strong sexual and emotional language by the characters as they discover their sexuality. It's important to remember that not every LGBT person has the same experiences and this book is not meant to represent any actions of the LGBT Community as a whole.

If these subjects are unwanted or too sensitive for you to read, please look for the " * " symbol at the beginning of a paragraph. This will be a warning of the presence of these sensitive/sexual depictions. At the end of these scenarios will be " ** " This will allow you, the reader, to bypass any sensitive subjects while still enjoying the main story line.

I would prefer that you enjoy the book and learn from the stories without worrying about being exposed to something you don't feel comfortable reading. You, my readers, have my upmost love and respect and gratitude for all of your support. Without your love, this book and the books that follow wouldn't be possible.

J.R. Gray-Heim

Resources for LGBTQ

The Trevor Project
www.thetrevorproject.org
Founded in 1998 by the creators of the Academy Award®-winning short film TREVOR, The Trevor Project is the leading national organization providing crisis intervention and suicide prevention services to lesbian, gay, bisexual, transgender, queer & questioning (LGBTQ) young people under 25.

Equality NC
www.EqualityNC.Org
Equality North Carolina is the oldest statewide organization in the country dedicated to securing rights and protections for the LGBTQ community.

HRC Human Rights Campaign
www.hrc.org
The Human Rights Campaign envisions a world where every member of the LGBTQ family has the freedom to live their truth without fear, and with equality under the law.

Fayetteville Pride
www.fayettevillepride.org
Our mission is to instill pride, celebrate unity, and embrace diversity and inclusiveness in our LGBTQ* community and allies, and to provide a support network and educational advocacy group dedicated to increasing awareness and acceptance.

Chapter One

Growing up in an extremely religious family that was heavily involved in the church - it's only fitting that most of my adolescent years were filled with memories of youth camps, teen events and lots of "Hellfire and brimstone" preaching. My mind was crammed with a fundamentalist Christian religious doctrine from a young age. My father - a former preacher himself - was looking for a new church for our family to attend. The search had begun for our "Church Family." And if you're from the south - you know which church you are a member of is just as important as which college you graduated from.

I was a newly slim 15 year old, who was finally able to throw away the notorious Levi's® Husky jeans from 2 years earlier. I had short, front spiked up black hair and pewter framed wired glasses. I personally hated having to change churches. That meant being forced to meet new people, which was never a strong skill of mine. Barely reaching 5'7; I was the typical nerdy, average American kid with a bit more style than most guys my age.

Our family was of a lower income; living paycheck to paycheck and didn't have the money for expensive clothes. My mother would always find a family with kids older than us, so we constantly had a stream of hand-me-downs. My wardrobe depended on what was in those bags. Luckily, this time the hand-me-downs came from a family that had money and the bags were filled with name brand clothes. I didn't even care if they were worn before or not exactly my size; it was all name brand and being able to wear expensive clothes at that age meant an immediate increase in social standing in my small Southern town.

In our search for a new Church Family, we pull up to a church with "A" frame architecture and massive medieval style, ten-foot front doors, flanked by narrow tinted windows on either side and above. Opening the massive door for my mother, struggling under the sheer weight of the solid, almost unmovable door, my father reaches over my head to speed up my gentlemanly obligations and allow my mother and younger sister Emmalee to walk under his arm. Leaving the full weight of the door to push me into the expansive room and slam behind me. I gather myself from the near fall and I survey the wide vestibule that is swarming with church goers hustling and bustling between small groups and the welcome table which is placed between the two sets of double doors. The variety of women's perfume mixed with equally stout Brut made me cringe and my nostrils flare. Wall-to-wall mauve pink carpet with massive brick accent wood pillars encased three pairs of light wood grained half etched glass paned swinging doors. Through each pane of glass I could see the auditorium style sanctuary with mauve pink carpet and velour upholstered pews. God, it looked like the Holy Ghost came down and blew Pepto-Bismol everywhere.

We were greeted by my Aunt Leslie, who broke herself away from a gaggle of women near the far door, with Uncle David in tow; both 12 years senior to my dad. My uncle standing in his perfectly pressed grey suit and red tie, stood a few inches taller than me. His salt and pepper hair was always in a swept up combover hairstyle, sprayed into perfection by multiple layers of Rave hairspray. As I look at Uncle David, I notice that where his pocket square normally would be was a plastic burgundy clip that spelled out DEACON in bold white letters. My aunt, who was on his left, was already in mid hug with my mother. Aunt Leslie was flowing around in a turquoise pleated dress with an oversized collar, matching open toe heels and a long dangly grouping of gold toned necklaces. As she made her way to me, she hugged me as the corners of her dress collar, sharp from the years of over starching and heavy perfume scratched my face. Her Princess Diana style hair, perfectly feathered back, bounced as she grabbed our hands and led us through the set of double doors into the sanctuary. Following her lead, my mother latches her grip on my hand and pulls me to our family's place in the numerous rows of pews. As any good Southern Baptist knows; you have to respect the unspoken seating chart. Accidentally sitting where the Barnes family has sat for five generations wouldn't be a good idea, so we were grateful for Aunt Leslie's direction.

Sitting next to my sister, the room around us was buzzing with churchgoers greeting, laughing, and having conversations while the overly enthusiastic pianist played a classic hymn on the grand piano that is tucked into the right of the choir loft. This church with the mauve carpeting and massive doors was a stark difference from the previous forty person small room church we had attended since I was four years old. This church could easily sit over three hundred people, with room to spare. Noticing the incredible height of the cathedral ceilings, my awe was interrupted by a loud finger snapping. My aunt abruptly ended my trance of staring at the tall white and gold paned rectangle chandeliers, hanging directly over my head.

"You guys are here on one of the most perfect Sundays. We have a new pastor starting today and his son is around your age, Van. I'll make sure to introduce you two boys after you break out for teen services."

"Teen Services?" I asked, while giving my mother a frustrated look.

"Yes! We all are together for opening prayer and singing and then the teens leave and have their own service in the brand new full size gymnasium!" Exclaimed my aunt Leslie, teetering between excitement and bragging. My aunt was very ostentatious and loved anything to do with showing off and appearances. My uncle enabled her notions by always making great money and Aunt Leslie was forever going on about what she was buying or doing anytime my mother was in earshot.

Before having the chance for clarification on the Teen Services, Uncle David and my father joined us, making all of us slide down the pew to make room. While doing the "Church Pew Shuffle", a combination of standing, moving slightly over, sitting, and standing again, my knees slam into the back of the pew in front of me. The loud bang prompted a rotund grandmother-like woman to turn around. "Hey babydoll, that sounded like it hurt," with a strong Southern lazy draw. "They want to make sure we're all on top of each other here." Her tone was warm and caring; a stark contrast to my aunt's shrill, birdlike yapping. "It makes the horrible singing from Maebelle back yonder less noticeable." Pointing her arthritic hand to the back corner of the sanctuary to a six-foot tall Amazononian looking woman, draped in what can only be described as something hanging in Elvis' jungle room.

"I swanny, I doubt she's got a full length mirror in her house," the older lady snidely smirks. "Trust me, you'll hear her loud caterwauling as soon as the music starts!" And with her last dig, her entire body jumped with laughter as she turned her back to me, facing the pulpit and choir loft. Turning around to catch a glimpse of Ms. Amazonion again, I'm greeted by a pinch on my arm from my mother, accompanied by a look all of us know too well. The look of, "you know better than that, and you better act right, or else!"

Moving to position myself as comfortably as I can with a still lingering stinging knee from the pew's impact, and now a burning "church-pinched" arm, I find myself dead center in the massive room just as everyone starts standing and music starts blasting over the PA system. In my distractions, I hadn't noticed the music minister approaching the pulpit, leaving me the only one seated among the standing congregrents. I cautiously rise while taking extra care not to hit my knees again or exchange pleasantries with the older woman; something I desperately wanted to prevent from happening again. At that moment, I knew I had to participate because in a Southern church - just like in Southern life - appearance and participation was everything.

Chapter Two

    Standing in the vast crowd of people, unsure of what to expect, a projection screen drops over the two story baptismal as the glowing song lyrics appear, and the music director starts. The songs and general feel of Heritage Baptist was more upbeat and modern than our last church, and frankly, I found it to be more enjoyable. I knew some of the songs and with the entire church erupting in prompted directional cues from the music minister; I felt oddly comfortable and started to sing with the group.

    In my singing, I recalled the comments about Ms. Maebelle and her apparent bad singing. I quietly quit my own singing, straining my ears to the back of the room, which immediately confirmed the older lady's comments. Billowing from the back pews was a combination of sounds similar to that of a woman's agony in childbirth or a cow in heat. Definitely not the best singing, but quite amusing nonetheless. The song ended with echoes of "Amen's!" And "Hallelujahs", reaching from every corner of the room while everyone sat down. This went on for three songs, standing up and sitting down each time. This was playing hell on my swollen knee but I complied for family appearance purposes. Having a sore knee was better than a black and blue arm, the markings from repetitive "church pinches" given out by my mother.

Finally, the last song allowed me to rest my knee and get comfortable as the music director waved at the front pew to a dark haired, tan, man. This man stood next to a red haired petite woman, dressed in a tasteful two piece blue and cream suit skirt combination, looking very statuesque. Leaning over, she instructed her four children to stand with them, turning to give a friendly wave to the eager congregation.

"Everyone, today is a joyous occasion," stated the out of breath music minister, with a sense of pride in his voice. Still out of breath from having the stage all to himself for a concert-like performance of four songs and the energetic waving of his arms. Swallowing thickly to catch his breath, he continued, "Today we welcome our new Pastor, Rich Davis and his wife Ms. Denise, to our church family, along with their four kids, Ruth Ann and Gwyneth (twins), Mary and their only son, Jeremiah". I stretched my neck to peer around the older lady's teased up beehive, trying to get a better look at who they were talking about.

They were a gorgeous family. Pastor Rich and Ms. Denise looked like they were straight out of a Macy's catalogue, perfect features with brilliant white smiles. Mary was to her mothers right and was the oldest. Looking to be about seventeen years old, she was taller than average for her age. Beside Mary were Ruth Ann and Gwyneth, the youngest of the group. The twin girls dawned matching ringlet curls and white ruffled shirts and royal blue sweaters and plaid skirts. And on the end of the pew, closest to the aisle was Jeremiah. He looked to be between his sisters in age, he looked to be around my height, though it was hard to tell with the concert hall style slanted floor of the sanctuary.

Having the most room to move, Jeremiah eased into the aisle as they were all waving and smiling, trying their hardest to make the best impression. The chandelier above him, identical to the one above my head, made his blonde hair glisten like ocean waves being kissed by a glimpse of the morning sunrise; giving him an almost angelic aura around him. His aura was nothing compared to his steel blue eyes, perfectly grey blue dots surrounded by luscious full dark lashes. His frame displayed his athletic stature with his clothes clinging to his body, showing a toned, swimmers build. Wearing a freshly pressed, tight-fitting red and white checkered button up long-sleeved shirt, and a tight rope-style necklace, with one small white shell in the center dangling over a predominant Adam's apple.

The small shell of the necklace looked like a pearl next to his naturally tan skin, as it lifted and fell with each wave of his hands to the overly excited church members. I found myself lingering on him for what felt like an eternity; unaware of anyone else but him. His shirt was perfectly tucked into slim cut khakis, making him look as though he was dipped in wax to form the fabric. The folds of each pocket and how muscular yet slim his body was. Sheer perfection, I knew this boy was handmade by no one other than God.

As the applause started to end, the family turned back around as Pastor Rich approached the pulpit. Lifting his jacket, he flicked on a small box which was obviously placed prior to the beginning of church, wasting no time to introduce himself as he narrowed the gap between him and the stage. Clutching a worn maroon red leather Bible in one hand, he placed his free hand on the pulpit, turning to face the eager flock. His voice was commanding but welcoming - not extremely Southern like my family but just enough of a drawl to his voice to know he was from the south. I see my Aunt Leslie grinning like the Cheshire Cat, eager to enjoy this long awaited day.

During Pastor Rich's opening prayer and the sharing of his family's history, I was checked out mentally. I was thinking of his son, Jeremiah when he asked for us to bow our heads and close our eyes; I kept my eyes open looking straight ahead at the large cross hanging on the back wall behind the choir loft, draped with various colors of silk fabrics. I felt the judgment of the cross burning in my eyes while I pondered what exactly was happening to me. Up to this point I had never had any thoughts or attractions to anyone other than the occasional girl in class, but never a guy. Now all these feelings were surfacing that had either been shoved away by too many "HellFire" sermons or just simply naivety.

I was attracted to Jeremiah, but that was wrong! My mind goes back a few months, standing at the checkout line at Winn-Dixie, and hearing my mother and father discuss some of the magazines that were displayed on either side of the candies and chewing gum. "You know that just ain't right!", my father balked as he grabbed a magazine from the stack. Waving it in front of my mother to show his disdain. "You tell me, what's next? Forcing our children to watch homosexuals parading on Sesame Street? Not in my house! No sirree! My hand to God, our home will never be a place where perversion is celebrated!"

Ending his tirade with my mother, who simply shrugged, trying to organize her coupons for a speedy checkout, he leaves us standing in the grocery store to wait in the minivan, leaving me and my mother to handle the bags. After his huffing, I looked at the magazine, curious about what had him so riled up. In big bold print, "YEP, I'm Gay!" On a picture of Ellen Degeneres, who I only knew because my mother watched every episode, except the previous Wednesday. I just figured the show ended, but apparently, she had revealed who she was; my parents weren't having any association to anyone or anything that promoted homosexuality.

Before I could connect any of my feelings from the Time Magazine memory to the present, the teens were dismissed to the Teen Service. Realizing I was in the middle of the pew, I stood and committed to the tedious yet methodical side step, through the family's crowded pew, to reach the aisle. Once there, I was completely lost on where to go, or what to do from there.

"Honey, stop looking like a deer in headlights and just follow the group", barked my mother, looking at my sister and I, with the focused beam of her eyes burrowing deep into my forehead. This "Mother's look" was usually used for pulling the truth out or putting the fear of death on anyone's shoulders, it could also direct you quickly to make a fast decision. ***Classic Southern Mother Handbook Lesson One - Master a Look that Both Adds Fear but Also Keeps You Fom Using Words.***

"You listen now!" Saying quickly, before the congregation had time to settle, "meet us back right here once church is over. No lollygagging around! You're here for one purpose - to learn about God and remember what I can't see; he can." ***Southern Mother's Handbook Lesson Two - Fear with a Hearty Helping of Guilt.*** My mother was more than just the master of this lesson, she exuded guilt anytime someone was watching. A firm hand and sharp words were the way of the Shelton's for generations, and whatever my mother didn't dish out, it was open game for any of my aunts or uncles to take up the slack.

Chapter Three

Taking the lead with my younger sister in tow, we rush from the center aisle of the church to catch the other teens, before they disappear through the set of doors behind the grand piano. Crossing the threshold we form a herd into the maze of hallways that lead to the glossy maplewood doors. Both sides of the walls are covered in religious prints and the occasional "Bake Sale" notice. I chuckled quietly at how easily a reverent place could be graffitied with tacky hand drawn flyers and busy poster boards with glitter and marker strokes.

Reaching the back door of the church, lined up like worker ants marching to a dirt mound; we enter the newly constructed, two-story brick gymnasium located in the back corner of the parking lot. Looking back at the church and then again at the gymnasium I realize how out of place the new building seemed. It was a completely different style than the church and seemed more appropriate for a YMCA rather than a church but then again, I'm no architect. Shrugging my judgment away, we approach the entrance as I catch a glimpse of a group of teenage girls rushing about, full of laughter and mindless chatter; obviously trying to get a chance to sit next to the new pastor's son. As I look for a seat, the familiar scent of Clinique Happy cologne slaps me in the face. I close my eyes slightly, taking a long deliberate inhale, savoring the most luxurious teenage cologne, belonging presumably to Jeremiah. The citrus smell, only meant for the hottest of guys, and too expensive for me to own. The closest I had to Clinique were the magazine samples in one of the magazine's at the doctor's office.

The Teen Service was nice enough and went on as expected. A few older adults introduced themselves to us while playing matchmaker with the first-time visitors. The adults placed us with random teens as sort of a "Baptist Buddy System" putting me in a group of guys around my age. By the looks of it, most of my group were already best friends and I stood out as the lone sheep. I looked up from my frustration at being the odd one out and noticed Jeremiah was across the room with a smaller group of guys ironically mirroring the jock's table present in most school cafeterias. All of the popular girls were hanging on every word spoken by the guys, hoping for the slightest sign that one of the jocks might be interested in them.

My group was pleasant but full of the usual testosterone driven comments of hunting, the girls they thought were cute and the casual bet of who could touch the rim of one of the 2 basketball nets, situated on either end of the basketball court turned into a makeshift church. Finding a seat in the back, I waited for the impending sermon on being a good Christian servant for the Lord to begin and hopefully end just as quickly.

Sitting alone for a moment allowed me to replay the last 15 minutes in my head. "What the heck was going on? Why was I so intrigued by this guy?" He hadn't been in town a full day and already had droves of people around him at his beckoning call.

Then there's me. My mind starts fretting as I have this internal dialogue where I downplay the value of my presence and question if anyone would ever desire my infatuations. In my fog, I wanted to hurry this along, close my eyes for the closing prayer, and grab Emmalee's hand and head home as quickly as possible to allow the last remnants of this day to be salvaged. I assumed my parent's mind would be made before the minivan's tires rolled out of the crowded parking lot of Heritage Baptist.

I found my mother just as instructed after the Teen Service ended, tapping her shoulder to get her attention, as she is agreeing to attend this Sunday's evening ladies prayer group. Unintentionally, a louder than expected sigh rolls from my gut, not ignored by my mother. Her wrath would never be seen in public, but I knew better than to relax. I knew I would have to pay for that public display of misbehaviour in the minivan on the way home.

After an eternity of standing and patiently waiting, my father was able to peel my mother away right before she had the chance to volunteer the entire family to polishing each pew and window each day for the rest of our lives. Making a bee-line for the propped open front doors where my Uncle David was perched, shaking hands with people as they exited the church on their way home. My mother shifted lines with my sister and I in tow, ensuring she could steal a chance to introduce herself and her "picture perfect family" to the new pastor's family.

It felt like a funeral procession with the generic "we're so glad you came" and the occasional "we can't wait to hear more lessons from you", blah, blah, blah. I was ready to get in the minivan and get whatever punishment my mother handed down, over with. "What was I going to be grounded from this time?" I pondered, as my mother reached the front of the line.

"Hey Pastor, my name is Amelia Shelton and these are my children, Emmalee and Donavan." Knowing what was expected, I reached out a hand, like a true Southern gentleman, smiling at both the pastor and his wife.

"Y'all are the reason we came today. David and Leslie Shelton, my sister & brother-in-law, made sure to let us know when you were starting, so we could make the leap and join the church." My mother says, railroading her words with excitement. "Maybe we could get our kids together sometime if you want," saying in that as-a-matter-a-fact way she's known for. "That would be absolutely lovely Mrs. Shelton, we are still commuting from South Carolina while trying to find a house; but we may take you up on that offer," Ms. Denise replies quickly, a relieved sound in her voice, with the chance of having help with her children during the move. I knew better than to moan or mumble at being volun-told to be friends with the pastor's kids; I was already on thin ice and I didn't want to spend my week in a stripped down bedroom with only the slight hum of the ceiling fan keeping me entertained.

Annoyed, I just smile and listen as plans are made and my mother writes our number on the church bulletin and hands it to the pastor and his wife. My mother seemed accomplished in that moment, with a pep in her step as we walked through the parking lot to the family minivan. Selfishly, I hoped that her happiness would over run her memory of my outward sign of disrespect, while in the presence of others. Before heading home, Mom announced that we were swinging by Kmart to get some groceries and a few household items before making the twenty minute drive up the interstate to our home.

Chapter Four

Aimlessly, we walked down each aisle of the K-mart, back and forth, filling the cart with various items needed for the week. We ended up in the men's clothing department with my mother looking at a rack of possible new work shirts for my dad. I escaped the confines of holding the shopping cart and walked around the end-cap display of Wrangler Jeans. I needed a reprieve and I hoped to get two seconds of alone time before continuing on with my family. Looking up from my sluggish feet, I realize I'm standing in the middle of the men's underwear aisle. Frozen, as if seeing a ghost; unprepared for my reaction to this kind of stimuli.

This wasn't my first time in this aisle, quickly seeing the brand I put on as I was getting dressed this morning. However, now I was noticing more detailed varieties of styles and colors that I hadn't really paid any attention to before. Now I was examining each shelf in an almost methodical amazement from the top shelf to the bottom shelf. Each package displayed a perfectly tan and sculpted, over exaggerated male model wearing what was tightly folded in each displayed plastic package. I was oddly fascinated by the model's bodies and how the different underwear were showing off one very obvious feature. My cheeks began to heat up, when I looked at the pictures with the light color fabric which allowed more of the skin tones to show through. It fascinated me how the same guy could look so different in seven different styles of underwear yet I look the same no matter what. Photoshop… you evil bitch; making consumers think we will look just like the models. When I looked in the mirror I only saw a frumpy geek with brightly colored underwear. It was completely unfair! My daze ended with my mother calling out for me, signaling her defeat in finding my father any upgrades from his old oil-stained, blue button ups.

Why was my stomach swimming right now? Why did I have butterflies in my stomach? Trying to avert the attention of my parents, I hurried back to the cart and pushed it through the checkout line, then loaded the minivan with bags of the most random purchases. My mother wasn't the best shopper and this trip was no exception. Who buys bug spray, mouse traps, toothpaste, and Wonder bread then puts them in the same bag? Ughh. But these were not my monkeys, nor my circus; so I just say nothing and do as I'm told.

My father's off-key singing to Garth Brooks and my mother's attempt to keep up with The Dixie Chicks made the car ride home feel like an eternity. When we reach our neighborhood, it hits me; my mother's imminent scolding is coming and I doubt it will be pretty. The secret hope that she forgot quickly disappeared when she reminded me of our after lunch conversation while she was unloading the car. As we walked towards the house she said that I needed to work on my attitude in public. I sheepishly looked down at the gravel under my feet and received what could only be described as a sample of what was to come later on in the day.

Grateful to finally be alone in my room, I climbed into bed, with my eyes closed, feeling relieved to be in the one place that was just mine. What was I thinking and what the heck was going on? I questioned myself again, why had Jeremiah been so hypnotic and why did I notice the underwear aisle so differently today than ever before? Sleep soon found me, not caring that I was still in my church clothes. I drift off, as my brain tries to rationalize if I had a terminal brain injury or was just losing my mind. My worrying was short-lived as the thoughts of Jeremiah switched to forgotten dreams and snores.

The faint sound of my mother working away in the kitchen echoed down the hallway to my room. She gathered the ingredients for a Lemon Crumb coffee cake for the evening's prayer meeting, I was wishing she could make an extra one for dinner. I settled in my pillow and drew a long yawn with my arms encircling my case-less pillow. I roll over and grant my brain a much needed break from our 900 sq foot home. Sleep was the only way to escape the claustrophobia and forced interactions with my family.

I wasn't sure how long I was asleep when I cracked my left eye open; catching the sight of my mother sitting at the foot of my bed.

"Woooah! What the …. You scared me!" I gasped, while pulling my upper body against the headboard. Cautiously aware of what I almost said in front of my mother. "Van, honey we need to talk about what happened today," she says in a low, stern tone while holding back a smile.

She was a tough woman but also loved joking around. This made it hell trying to guess if she was serious or pulling you along for the punch-line. I hated being called "Van" and she knew it. Each generation of our family seemed more elaborate with their children's names, only to shorten them to a nickname that would be used instead of the actual given name. In any respectable Southern family if you heard your actual full government printed birth certificate name - your ass was going to get it or you knew that you better listen immediately. Southern Mother Lesson #15 - Use the full name only when needing to scare the hell out of someone.

I knew she was mad but I wasn't too worried because she didn't refer to me as "Donovan Andrew Shelton." I knew the look that burned my skin that morning wasn't a joke. I had embarrassed her in a public place while she was meeting new people and trying to make the best first impressions - "You know your father and I have had a really hard time trying to find a place for all us to belong since we left NorthStar Baptist." The heaviness of her words felt sad. "We didn't want to leave but the old money in that place kept it from growin' and we ain't sittin' back while all those old people refuse to try anything new with you youngins". Hearing her lazy southern accent would make you think she was a true southern belle; Nope! She was born in New Jersey. My grandfather moved her entire family down south when she was nine, she never claimed to be from the north. She preferred the term, "Converted Yankee," or as my dad would say, "A Damn Yankee."

Standing at the foot of the bed, towering over my sleep glazed eyes, she continues with her lecture, "Today, we found the place for us, and you go and show your attitude in front of everyone? What do you think that says about you? You're not a bad kid, just a kid with a horrible attitude anytime we ask you to do something. That has to change. And now!" Fiercely pointing down to the floor, almost stabbing the dot to an imaginary explanation point, she emphasises the importance of what's expected moving forward. "We are going to dive into this church and go to anything and everything they have goin' on. You complained about NorthStar being boring and having nothing for kids, now we've made the change. Then you go and give me an attitude on the first day there? Not gonna fly buddy." Now with her hands, clenched into fist on her hips, leaning forward as I slowly cower down into my mattress, feeling the heat of her voice, push me into submission.

"We've made the change?" Confused, I ask, wondering how long I've been asleep since I missed the family discussion on joining the church. While walking out of my room my mother offers a small laugh, "Yep, we made the change and joined. You must have slept through when we voted, so that makes your vote an automatic YES!" She utters in a playful way, "Before we left I grabbed flyers for all the activities and a schedule for the teen events and services. Make sure to look at the kitchen calendar to see what's going on because you're going to be busy; and you'll love it!" Announcing as she continues down the hallway to the kitchen, her voice trailing as she rounds the corner to the living room. This was her classic way of ending a conversation with the last word - walk away while talking, removing the ability for anyone to talk back or protest.

Chapter Five

The chaotic schedule of Heritage Baptist became our new routine. We started each morning checking the calendar of events newsletter that was stuck to the refrigerator door. Heaven forbid, my mother missed a chance to volunteer us for something, or send my sister and I to a teen outing playing laser tag. Though church technically was on Sunday, we pulled into that asphalt parking lot six days a week.

Spring had long passed as the humidity of summer rolled into the valleys of North Carolina. The azalea bushes surrounding the front doors of Heritage Baptist, previously pink and white, were now brown, baking under the July sun. School may have been out for the summer, but church continued on with services every Sunday; both morning and evening. There was teen devotional study and a small church service every

Wednesday night, after mom got home from work. Meetings and Bible lessons were every Thursday night followed by dinner in the church gym. Youth outings, usually putt-putt or bowling, happened on Friday nights. And the occasional cookout on Saturdays with friends from my parents' Sunday school class. Going to church was almost a full time job and I was ready for a day off.

"Donavon, What size shoe do you wear? And how tall do you think you are?" My mother beckoned from the living room. Sitting at my computer, bouncing between friends on AOL Instant Messenger, leaning back in my chair, I yelled across the hall, "I think I'm about six foot tall, Why?" Laughter exploded, echoing down the hall, "Honey, they ain't no way you're six foot tall, more like 5'6!" Still laughing at my lapse of judgment, she continues, "and you wear the same size shoe as your daddy, right?", being just brass enough to hurt my pride. "Yes mom, I think so. Size 10. Why?" I asked again. "We have to go to Dr. Kennedy's tomorrow morning, so make sure you shower and get up by 8am." still ignoring my initial question. Frustrated, I ask again, raising my voice, trying to get her to hear me, "Mom! Why? What are you talking about?" As the question escaped my lips, I could hear my mother making her way down the hall to my room by the distinctive house-shoe shuffle of her slippers. "Because you have to have a physical for soccer." Giving a playful emphasis to the word soccer she leans into the door frame of my room, half her body still in the hallway, "SOCCER?" I said, snapping up from the computer screen with a cringed bewildered look at my mom, now dawning a shit-eating grin.

"Yes, practice starts next week for the fall season and all of your friends are joining the Baptist's League. And before you say anything, the check is already written and you're doing it!" Turning in a flash, she's shuffling back down the hallway, giving no option for me to protest.

"Jeremiah, Seth, Colby, and Brandon are all already signed up. You will love it." Making her way back to the kitchen, her words dance off the floor and walls as she pours herself a glass of lemonade from the fridge. Frantically running down the hall to catch her, all but yelling, trying to remind her that I've never even watched soccer much less played it.

Everyone who knows me knows I'm more of the bookworm/music geek type with no athletic bones in my body. "This is going to end badly mom, broken legs, arms, fingers…you name it." Begging my mother with the best pity-party, pouty production I could muster up. "Please don't make me do it!" Grabbing onto the back of her shirt, pulling it down like a toddler throwing a fit, launching my acting with a full pushed out bottom lip and fake sobs. "Stop! You'll stretch my good house shirt and God knows those McDonald's apple Pies are already doing enough damage to it." Giving no attention to my pleading while swatting at my hands. "You are going to do it whether you like it or not!" My performance had apparently failed me, and she had made my decision for me.

Feeling defeated, I storm off to my room and slam the door, knowing at this point I was beating a dead horse. I was yet again, volun-told. My summer would now be a daily collection of getting prepared to practice soccer; running drills, kicking balls, and honestly, not having any fun. The only remotely pleasing thing about this was Jeremiah was going to be on my team.

Over the past few months, he had created his own group within the teen group and unofficially assumed the role as their leader. Everyone was still very nice, the similarity between them and the "Cool Kids' in any American high school was uncanny. However, this group was slightly different. Jeremiah always made a point to involve me and invited me along, each time making me feel special and included.

However, the first few times he asked me to sit with them; I reluctantly declined. Truthfully, I was too scared. I expected them to do what most of the "cool kids" do; make fun of me or make me their gopher. Constantly having to prove my worth by doing the stupid stuff they didn't want to do and in turn they might grant me the smallest chance of being in their circle. I was no newbie to this. But to my amazement and relief; I couldn't have been farther from the truth. After his persistence each week for a month, I finally agreed to join them, only to realize that I fit right in. I learned Jeremiah was older than me, he loved reminding everyone of his seniority even if it was only by three months. He loved messing around and when the adults weren't around, telling dirty jokes. Mind you, we are strict baptists, the jokes were barely PG-13 by normal standards, but still risqué to us. But his jokes were never at the expense of someone else, especially the select few of us that were "The Guys".

My tantrum was interrupted by a familiar high pitched *doo doop* sound from the computer speakers. Looking at the grainy computer screen, a slight smile crept across my face when a familiar sports themed screen name appeared.

SPORTZ4U2NV: Hey man! Wassup?

It was Jeremiah. I start typing out a massive dramatic monologue of "woe is me's", until I realize how much that made me sound like a whiner, so I backspace the typed message and give a basic response instead.

TREBLEMAKER16: N2M u?

SPORTZ4U2NV: just chillin. You excited about soccer?

TREBLEMAKER16: I just found out about it. I'm stoked.

Completely lying! I just didn't want to be a buzz kill and make him think I was a dork.

SPORTZ4U2NV: Awesome! I think my dad said we're going to have a meeting at my house this weekend with the team. I think Colby's dad is our coach. He's awesome!

Colby's dad, Thomas, was an extreme fitness junkie. 6'4, muscles everywhere, the occasional lingering faded tattoo, proof that he had a wild streak earlier in his life. All of this was before finding God and becoming the head deacon for Heritage Baptist. All in all - I knew he was going to work our asses off.

TREBLEMAKER16: Sweet! We will be there! I warn you now, my mom will probably bring her Jello Salad. Warn the others! It's horrible!

SPORTZ4U2NV: LOL! Don't have to worry about me touching that! I'll stash some snacks in my room for reserves! Ttyl.

A thunderous sound of a door opening and closing echoed through the computer speakers, signaling that Jeremiah had logged off. Frustrated with my inability to be truthful about not wanting to play soccer, and lying to a friend, I switch the monitor off and bow my head.

In that simple exchange of words, my anger had subsided into a mere discomfort while walking back to the living room. Finding my mother and father in their usual spots on either side of the sofa. "Ok, you win! I'll do it. Sheepishly, flopping on the opposite loveseat to my parents. "But you know this is not going to be pretty. I don't even know one thing about soccer." "As if it was a choice" my dad mocks while keeping his gaze locked on the TV. Aimlessly flipping through channels on the tv, a condescending look plastered across his face. "Son, you'll be just fine. Everyone that signs up gets on the team. And you've got a good coach. I bet he'll make sure to whip your butt from being a sissy to an Allstar!" His words stabbed at my chest. Fighting back tears from yet another jab from my father, I cross my arms and shut my mouth. Not wanting to protest, unsure of what insult I would get next.

Watching tv with my parents, I zoned out into my own world of worries, the off and on faint noises from the tv show my father was watching playing in the background. I didn't want to play soccer, but I had no choice, so I might as well give it a shot. Maybe my father would actually be happy. If I'm really that bad; they just won't make me play. I'll get a jersey, get some sun, and get to hang with "the guys" all summer.

"Mom, Jeremiah said something about a meeting at his house this weekend, are we going?" Asking my mom, now in the kitchen, washing the dishes from dinner. "Well, of course honey! I've already got the Jello mold in the fridge - surprise! This one has something new in it", she says, pride beaming in her voice. My mother's "famous" Jello mold usually consisted of some type of fruit combination mixed with an array of nuts and berries which were suspended in a brightly colored gelatinous ring. She never ran out of ideas for the quivering gelatin dish; no matter the occasion.

Last Thanksgiving, she tried to spring a new surprise on the entire family with a Jello salad block. Celery, carrots, cheese and pecans were floating in a shiny orange goo with what looked to be mayonnaise smeared on the top. Dressing the plate, she arranged lettuce leaves with generous dollops of cottage cheese and crackers. They say that a Jello mold has its place on the dinner table whether as an appetizer, main course or a dessert. That was true for the Thanksgiving meal because no one touched the jiggling brick of vomit, no matter how many times my mother offered a slice.

Trying to avoid an embarrassing stand off between her kitchen creations and my friends' unprepared stomachs, I knew I had to steer her away from anything crazy being her contribution to the party. "Oh God! Mom, not another one? I say jokingly, looking at my father for any sign of agreement. "I never understand how you're supposed to eat one of those. Do you cut it like a cake or scoop it like ice cream - NO ONE KNOWS?" Lifting both arms up, giving a dramatic confused look.

Acting as though I wasn't speaking, my mother continued washing dishes, rinsing and placing them in the dish rack. Knowing my cue, I retired back to my bedroom, bored with nothing to do. Logging back into AOL to kill some time before bed, I get greeted by the friendly, "You've Got Mail", making my eyes roll into the back of my head. "Probably some Junk mail" I thought while reading through the list of Vacation Offers, Magazine Subscription Advertisements and then there was an actual personal email; from Colby's Dad, Mr. Thomas - well, now my Coach Thomas.

Hey Guys!

I'm excited to start the Heritage Baptist Church Soccer Team this year and can't wait to see all you guys showing just what you're made of. Not just in skill but in Christian values and teamwork. Practices will be held every Tuesday and Thursday night at 7pm at the City Rec. Center, field 3 - starting Aug 28th. Games will be Saturday mornings at approximately 11am starting September, lasting through November. Playoffs will be the weekend before Thanksgiving - I know we can make it

all the way to the top! The schedule is still subject to change.

Items to bring:
Water bottle, Cleats, Towel, Soccer Ball, Shin pads, Knee Guards, Long Socks, Athletic Cup (optional),

We will be running drills and will work on team positions within the first few practices. Start thinking of what position you want to play and we will see if we can make that happen.

In Christ,
Coach Thomas

Holy lord! That's a lot of stuff! We didn't have the money to spend on getting everything I needed, and I doubt it would be easy to find these things second hand. I was always aware of our family's financial struggles - more than any child should be. My parents openly talked about it at the kitchen table most nights. Guilt began to flood my stomach as I tried adding in my head at how much all the equipment would be. I guess I know what everyone will be getting me for my birthday next month; soccer gear that I didn't even want. So much for a new computer any time soon.

Hitting reply, I sent off a basic response:

Thank you coach, I'm looking forward to learning more about soccer. I've never played before, so whatever position you think I'll do best; I'd be open to try.

Thanks!
Donovan Shelton

Secretly, I wondered if the waterboy position was filled? Knowing that would be the only position I was remotely capable of without looking like a total dweeb, and the only position I was qualified for in my father's eyes.

Chapter Six

Carefully balancing the gelatinous goo on a tray in my lap, we make the turn into the prestigious "Glenndover Hills - North" neighborhood. Feeling out of place in our two toned, ten year old, used minivan; we were greeted by overly manicured lawns with pristine bushes and huge displays of southern indulgences. Every driveway had the same style cast iron mailbox with bright gold numbers; some flanked with blue iris or bright pink and red camellia bushes.

"Holy crap mom!" I exclaimed, pointing with my free hand at a massive Georgian colonial in the bend of the road ahead of us. Seeming as though it was growing as we continued our drive, getting more and more impressive as we kept pace around the turn. "That thing looks like a college!" Gasping, while turning my head slowly as we passed the final of twelve columns that held multiple stories above a stone veranda. The massive columns were situated in front of row-after-row of black shuttered windows, giving a "Gone With The Wind" vibe. "Watch your mouth!" My mother snapped, unfazed by the presence of such grandeur. "Honey, thou shalt not envy thy neighbor" as she looked left and right at each mailbox, looking for our destination in a part of town, rarely seen by us. Rounding the next curve, the homes kept going and getting closer together, getting slightly smaller; yet still with the same style of mailbox. About a mile into the neighborhood; nestled in a row of live oak trees with wide-magnificent arching branches that formed rounded canopies of shade to shelter the brightly colored azalea bushes, was 2293 Overbanks Drive.

A modest, pale yellow and white 2 story home with attached two car garage. The front door tucked in the center of a partial wrap around porch with a big sign above scripted "The Davis Family" with Joshua 24:15 - As for me and my house, we will serve the Lord below. Four white rocking chairs evenly spaced, each with red pillows, monogramed with a capital "D". The front door was flanked by four sets of floor to ceiling windows framed in classic farm style black shutters. It beckoned a warm cozy retreat, welcoming everyone to enjoy the perks of prestige and status. In stark comparison to the others at the entrance of the neighborhood; theirs seemed more conservative however, still quite impressive.

Wasting no time, my mother hurried us to the front porch of Pastor Rich and Ms. Denise's country oasis. She passed me the now slightly melted horror of suspended fruit and pecans, (the surprise ingredient she was so excited to add). She looks back at me to make sure that I look presentable, takes a deep breath and rings the doorbell.

"Ms. Shelton! I'm glad you could find it, come on in honey and make yourself at home." Ms. Denise greets us, while rubbing her hands on her pleated red and white checkerboard ruffled kitchen apron. "You can call me Millie," mother's voice was higher than normal. "I always prefer it to Amelia." She was trying to narrow the gap from pastor's wife, to friend, I suppose. "Ok, Millie it is then. And I'm sorry son, what's your name?" Ms. Denise cheerfully says while releasing the cold Jello mold from my now numb hands. "My name is Donovan, ma'am." I say with a smile, looking at my mother, making sure she could see I was being respectful. "Now that's something I love, a young man with perfect manners. Sweetie, you just call me Denise" she says turning into the kitchen. My mother looks at me, with a full smile, leans into me, whispering through her teeth, trying not to be heard by the others in the living room, "You WILL call her Ms. Denise, not Denise, you understand." Nodding my head in agreement to deny our pastor's wife's request, I follow behind my mother, matching her steps as she meets Ms. Denise at the kitchen table.

Passing through the large vaulted living room, the fathers of my teammates were laughing and lazily sitting on the couches speaking quietly enough to keep their conversation private. While the kitchen was buzzing with high pitched chatter, ringing from every corner of the expansive rooms. The mothers were a stark difference to the men. Overly excited laughter mixed with the clanking and clattering of dishes, each woman talking over the next, trying to be heard; my head begins to spin at the shrill of the voices that are progressively getting louder and louder. Unsure of where to go, I stood in place until given further instructions from my mother and moved to invade the space in front of the sink.

"Honey, If you go past the fridge; that door leads to the basement, Jeremiah's room is down there." Using the caked up potato salad spoon as a pointer, Ms. Denise, obvious of my discomfort, "I think you're the last of the boys expected. Everyone will be excited to see you," Letting that last statement linger in my ears, I couldn't imagine anyone being excited to see me, but it had to be better than the torture I was getting by being in this kitchen.

Snapping out of my confusion, almost running, I grab the door, open it and immediately hear familiar voices echoing up the stairs from the basement. My gait suddenly halts and I take each step slowly, as if I was walking to my own execution. At the bottom of the stairs, in what seemed to be a large family room, I found all "The Guys." They are sitting around the brown leather sectional, which is situated in front of a massive flat screen projection tv. "Well, I'll be daggum!" Says Colby, standing from the center of the group, "he's actually going to do it!" Narrowing the space between me and the couch he throws his arm around me, pulling me into the conversation; making me bend to get under his shorter stature. The smell of freshly applied Degree deodorant and Abercrombie Fierce cologne (a scent that provokes sexiness to anyone who wears it) surrounded me. Without the cologne, you could be a three-out-of-ten, but with it, a solid ten. Colby's body leaned into mine, as his arm tightened around me, inching me down into a playful headlock. Not to hurt me, but in jest.

Colby was the youngest of our group, only a few months my junior, but shorter than me. Standing 5'5, looking like everyone's little brother; what he lacked in height, he made up for in muscles, everywhere. His teal blue American Eagle shirt was stretched over a perfectly sculpted chest with round pecs. Reaching out to connect to his veiny, chiseled arms, his sheer strength dwarfed my own, and began to stir something in my pants. I tried to release his touch on my body, and calm my growing betrayal, but was met instead with Colby's arm tightening and playfully tickling my sides. Liberating my neck from his grip, his arm falls, now cupping my shoulders, giving me a friendly, yet firm hug. Unsure of what to do, I allowed my arm to naturally go around his back, feeling that his muscles matched in definition and fullness to everywhere else on his body. All of his muscle gave him a full 360 degrees of brawn and a solidness to his shorter stature. This was the first time I had noticed how built he was; no surprise since his father was a regular at Gold's Gym. He was a strong contrast to my twiggy, slim, swimmer's body, wearing hand-me-down clothes that were obviously not my proper size.

Plopping me in the center of the sectional, I exchanged pleasantries while noticing one of the members of the "The Guys" was missing. "Where's Jeremiah?" I ask, looking around to see if I missed him in the cloud of testosterone. "Oh, he's still gettin' ready." Seth says, leaning over the coffee table while piling a chip with a heap of salsa. "Well, his daddy had him werkin' in the yard before we all got here and he was covered in red mud from head to toe", Seth laughs out loud, snorting at each laugh, before shoving the full chip into his mouth. Seth was the red-haired, average looking country-bumpkin of the group. Taller than all of us, reaching 6'0, and full of southern farm boy arrogance and charm. His parents owned a dairy farm outside of town and while having a conversation with him; it's easy to imagine banjos playing and someone scratching a washboard in unison.

Seth was the joker of our group; always poking fun at one of us and usually getting into trouble for doing something he learned from one of the many farm hands his father employed. "You shoulda seen 'em. Carolina Red clay all up and down him. That boy look like he done wrestled a grizzly bear and lost!"

The room was in an uproar as a door at the end of the hallway, past the bottom of the stairs, opened. Oblivious, "The Guys" grow in their laughter and quips, and it mirrors the noises upstairs in the kitchen from their mothers, trying to one-up each other with a better depiction of Jeremiah's pre-shower state.

Luckily for me, I noticed the door opening and saw Jeremiah was standing in the doorway of his bedroom. He was zipping his pants and fighting to get his right arm in the sleeve of his white and red raglan shirt. Tirelessly, losing the battle with each tug and adjustment he tried. Watching the struggle, I got a full uninterrupted view of his slightly chiseled stomach with strongly defined "v" hip muscles. His body skin tone was slightly lighter in color than his face and he had a small dusting of well-groomed curly hair at his navel that trailed below his waistband. This moment of watching played out in slow motion, giving me a chance to savor a glimpse of something I didn't know I yearned for.

Jeremiah starts approaching the guys while still trying to pull his shirt together and snaps a quick response, "Now you know you're full of it, Seth. Had I gotten in a fight with a grizzly?? The only grizzly I know is your ex-girlfriend!" The room erupts in a thunderous combination of clapping, hooping, and hollering raising the decibel even higher than the kitchen. Before Seth could respond, Jeremiah plopped on the sectional next to me and smiled exposing his freshly brushed sparkling white teeth. I met his friendly gaze with a full smile. My smile was larger than normal because of my nervous energy and it definitely lasted longer than it should have. I felt like I had a coat hanger in my mouth pushing the corners of my lips wider. Finally breaking the agony, Jeremiah starts talking to everyone effortlessly about what positions they wanted to play on the team and what we should expect for the unforeseeable future.

I was so struck by him that I couldn't hear the words he was saying. I could only see his lips move. I was unable to break my smile as I saw him work the room like a true team captain. Snapping back to reality; I tried to catch up to what was being said, faking an understanding with an occasional nod and smile. The guys all seemed far more experienced than I was, so I kept my mouth shut. I didn't want to be seen as the weakest link on the first day of being a team.

"Hey Van!" Jeremiah says while hushing everyone's chatter, "What position do you think you'd like to be in?" For some reason, hearing him call me Van didn't give me the same internal fumes as it did when anyone else called me that. "I uh.….I think…uh.." Stuttering, looking down at my feet, as if the answer to this proverbial test were written on the tops of my feet. In shame, I continued, "Um..actually…uh…I actually don't know. I've never played…" The room fell completely silent. Blank stares and zero movement from the previously overly rowdy bunch caused an immediate lump in my throat, as a bead of sweat started to roll down my forehead.

Breaking the silence, Jeremiah reassures my nerves, "Oh that's ok man, after a few practices, you'll get the hang of it." Patting me on the back, he consoles my angst as he continues, "If you're fast enough, you may even end up in front of the net, stopping the other team from trying to score. Who knows? But only if Colby does a good enough job keeping them away from our side!" Turning back to the previous conversation, Jeremiah starts arguing with Colby on why Jeremiah was the better choice on being the Forward in field position and Colby would be better off as a Midfielder.

Still completely lost and overrun with the flooding of new feelings, I stand and ask where the restroom is located. Pointing to the same door that I just watched him walk out of, Jeremiah offers up, "Use mine down here, sorry it's not the cleanest, but it will work." Walking through the doorway, I am greeted by a half-made bed flanking the back wall of his massive, dimly lit room. The bed was in between two mismatched nightstands, each littered with half-emptied water bottles, sports drinks and Pringles canisters. Following the still-humid air, I find a modest sized bathroom with double sinks and a standing shower. Shutting the door didn't just give me privacy – it stopped the rumble of noise coming from the other room.

Leaning over and staring into the left sink, I couldn't believe what was happening. It was all too much. Making new friends, getting involved in the church groups and now playing soccer this summer. Six months ago, I was just fine in my little bubble of solitude, not expecting anything exciting to happen. Now I knew that I didn't have any hope of returning to my personal bubble even if it was the only place that felt safe. Pushing the treachery away, my mind starts focusing on the source of my fear. All of these feelings and physical reactions. This newfound attraction. I had to figure out what the hell was going on in my brain! It wasn't normal, I had never felt like this before Heritage Baptist, or had I?

It wasn't the church; our family had been to countless churches when my dad was actively preaching. It was Jeremiah. I had never looked at guys the way I looked at him. To be honest, I couldn't think of another guy who looked as perfect as he did. His smile, his personality, his messy but still perfect hair. Everything seemed absolutely flawless about him. But why did I care? Why did I notice? And why couldn't I control my arousal? I didn't get these feelings with girls. I mean, I fantasized about what it would be like to have a wife and kids, but never giving a thought to the physical act of what it would take to have that. I didn't soar with emotion around girls, but all of sudden, I was feeling all these emotions with guys.

I started thinking about the odd feeling I had when I saw Jeremiah in church that first day at Heritage Baptist. I started resurfacing and replaying the memory in my mind. Here I was sitting in his hot and humid bathroom, with the scent of his Old Spice Body Wash still lingering and I was having a different kind of feeling. I could feel a confused stirring in my pants. What the hell? Was I actually getting turned on by this? I mean, I am a teenager, weeks from being sixteen, and any amount of movement or vibration sends shockwaves to that particular area. But this time, in my current state of mind; I couldn't be more unsure of what was going on. My body was reacting to my thoughts and I didn't even know how to stop it. I start to panic! There is no way I can go out there with "The Guys" and have a full on "Bonosaursus Rex" tenting through my thin cargo shorts. I'm screwed! I thought, staring like a deer in headlights at myself in the mirror.

Trying to calm my crotch from coming to life, I start imagining all of the gross things I can think of. Still unable to tame the storm happening in the confines of my waistband. I whisper to myself, "Bologna…spoiled milk, dog crap. I gag. Taking a test…um…gym class; oh no! That one didn't help…" Damnnit, nothing is working! Frantic to get a grip on my awkward situation; figuratively and most definitely not literally. "JELLO SALAD! That's it! Jello Salad!"

Picturing that disgusting monstrosity did the trick, as my raging boner finally started to recede. Sighing into the mirror at myself, "Holy Lord! That was a close one." Reaching over to flush the toilet, creating the illusion that I was just using the bathroom, I turned the water on for a second and splash my face with cold water, dry my hands on the towel hanging by the sink and walk back out to join everyone. The guys were in the same place I left them, with no real decisions made on team positions. They were just agreeing that it wasn't our decision anyways, it was Coach Thomas' choice. Relieved to get a handle on my manhood's betrayal, I sit down at the far end of the sectional, allowing myself to calm down just as Ms. Denise calls us up for dinner. Finally, this night was moving on and hopefully I would be home before any other bodily malfunctions happened, wanting to prevent any more embarrassment from occurring in my new Pastor's home.

Chapter Seven

It seemed like everyday was filled with something new because of Heritage Baptist. A new feeling, or a new experience, I just wanted a routine, something to allow me time to figure out what was causing my needs and urges to change. I was tired of every interaction at the church, or with members of the church, being a surprise or something I hadn't planned.

Arriving at church for Sunday morning service, our family waits in the vestibule, while my parents chat with some of the other church members. Before we were able to reach the main sanctuary, a hand grabbed me, pulling me through the side door. I wasn't sure who had pulled me in the hallway, until the door shut behind me. "Man! Why didn't you say anything?" clearly frustrated, Colby punches my shoulder. "You didn't say anything about your birthday being tomorrow, and I had to hear it from my mom on the way to church!" Confused, and pissed that everyone would now know. "I honestly don't care about birthdays man! We don't usually..." My words stop. "Wait! How the heck did your mom know?" Questioning my abductor, clearly realizing he had been busted. "I, uh, well…I think my mom and your mom", Colby says, darting his eyes, trying to save his ass from busting the big secret. "You know something and you better come clean now or I swear to God…" My threat was interrupted by my mother, now in the doorway, giving "the look" to Colby. It felt awesome knowing that it wasn't me for once.

"You boys better hurry to Youth Church before they shut the doors! You don't want to be caught messing 'round the halls and get in trouble" she says, still not releasing her eyes from Colby. "Uh, yes Ma'am!" Colby belts, "We will go right now, Thank you Ms. Shelton." Grabbing my jacket sleeve, Colby drags me down the corridor to the back exit to the gymnasium. Unable to break his pull, feeling like a rag doll under his full control. "Col, if you don't tell me what the heck…" Freezing in the doorway of the gymnasium, I see the faint flicker of balloons bouncing, causing my cheeks to rush with color. "Shit!" I gruff under my voice, not loud enough for anyone to hear. "What have you guys done?" Grabbing Colby with my free hand, looking deep in his soul, angry that no one told me. "I hate surprises", rolling my eyes, trying to turn to walk back into the main building, blocked by Colby's grip.

"Look! Your mom and dad told our parents to get us here early." Colby confesses, realizing everyone had been found out. "We all brought snacks and Ms. Denise even got you a cake." Peering over Colby's shoulder, I try to get a preview before being forced through the door to the unwanted screams of my impending birthday surprise. "You know my parents Col," begging for sympathy for the one person tasked to bring me into the party. "This party is just to show off, they never do anything big for my birthday, this is just to show the church, that.." Stopping myself, realizing I was about to spill family secrets to Colby. "Let's just say, if they weren't trying to fit in so much, there would be no party, not anything like this." Unwavering, Colby reassures me again, that it will be ok, and that everyone wants to celebrate. "Man! It's your sixteenth birthday! This is a big day, just for you." And with that, we open the door to everyone jumping out, screaming "SURPRISE!"

Though the anger of my parent's forcing yet another experience on me was boiling in my eyes, I managed a smile to everyone as they ran to greet me with hugs and pats on the back. "Happy Birthday Van! You finally caught up to me," in jest, Jeremiah says, while leaning in to give me a hug. His shoulder catching under my chin as a lock of his hair tickles my nose. Instinctively, I inhale; bringing the scent of him into the depths of my soul. A tingle begins to stir in my pants as our bodies pressed together. Knowing what would follow, I pushed him off, trying to compose myself so that the possibility of what could have happened, wouldn't.

"Oh! We got you good? Didn't we?" My father says, pinching my cheeks with a mocking grin. "We knew this would be the best place to surprise you and your little friends were so excited to help. "You guys did amazing! Thank you all for doing this for us," he yells to everyone, as they start clapping. "Coming to Heritage Baptist was probably…no, it WAS the best decision me and Millie could have made." This was my father's failed attempt at making a speech. "We worried about how our kids would do, and if they would make friends, and luckily, we have all you guys."

"For us?" I thought to myself. How is my birthday party for us? Isn't it supposed to be for me? "It's hard to believe this little guy is sixteen! You know what that means? It means I'm getting old! Almost time to put me in the home!" In the classic Shelton way - you do something for someone else, but make the situation about you. I knew it! This party wasn't for me, it was for my parents to look good in front of my friends, in front of their friends. Frustrated, I pull away from my family and sit next to Jeremiah and Colby, at a table sprinkled with confetti and "Happy Birthday" napkins.

"You guys could have warned me!" I snapped. "And how would that have been a surprise?" Came a voice from behind Jeremiah. Leaning over the table, Daphne sits a clear plastic glass of soda and a small piece of cake on the table before she joins the group. "I know what a surprise is, but friends should always give me a heads up, it's just plain polite!" I say, not wanting to be lectured on being thankful or how I should act. "I tried to tell mom this was a bad idea, but your mom was relentless!" Colby says, placing an arm around my shoulders, giving me a comforting nudge. "Seriously! We know how you feel about things like this, but they wanted to do it, and we couldn't stop them." Enjoying the few moments I had about me, I give a sincere "Thank you" to the guys as my dad walks up behind me.

"Well, you're turning into a man right before my eyes!" My father sneers, placing a hand on either shoulder from behind me, squeezing hard enough to make me jump. "Boys, did I ever tell you about how Van used to…" Before he could finish making fun of me, I jumped up from the table, forcing him to release my shoulders and stop talking. The last thing I wanted was my father trying to be cool by throwing his only son under the bus, making fun of me in front of my friends. My father always thought telling embarrassing stories, or doing anything to make people laugh with him on my behalf was ok. It wasn't ok. But it was, like my mother kept telling me, "It's how your father says I love you." Why couldn't he just say it without it containing a punch line. "I'm going to get some cake!" I say, slamming my chair under the table, marching to the table that held my birthday cake, which was now being distributed around the room.

Taking a moment, I lean on the side table where my mother was tirelessly working to plate the cake and ice cream for the hoard of teens. I was getting more and more frustrated by the constant poking of my father, as a hand tapped me on the shoulder, causing my gaze to move from my feet to the broad frame of Coach Thomas. "Hey son! Happy

Birthday!" He says outreaching his hand to shake mine. "Thank you Coach, I appreciate it!" Lying through my teeth at this visual display of my family's dysfunctions. "Honey, I'm going to go sit this on the table for you if you want it. I hope you know that we love you, and I know you don't care about being the center of attention, but you will always be my baby and the center of my world." My mother says, blowing me a kiss, as she walks a plate over to where I was sitting. Stealing my father from my chair at the group of teens, forcing him to sit with the adults.

Coach Thomas continues, "I've never been a party person really, but I can say this, you are loved my friend." Loved? I look confused at Coach Thomas. Reading my face like a book, he picks up on my sheer madness of the situation. "I know you probably don't see it, but all these teens are here to celebrate you. Don't worry about your parents. They try the best they know how, and regardless of how they may do things wrong; at least they try. And sometimes they even miss the mark." Coach Thomas says, leaning to make sure his sentiments were only heard by me. "I know what you're feeling, my old man is the same way. But I promise you, eventually it gets easier. You have to trust me, even though your parents may have had the wrong idea about what this day is for," turning my body away from the table, giving a small gesture to the round table with half of the soccer team. "Those guys love you for who you are, and they would never try to steal your thunder like that, on or off the field."

Chapter Eight

The first few practices were basically 90% exercise/endurance and 10% actual soccer playing, and I still had no idea what I was doing. What I had learned rather quickly is: my shins would never be the same again. On the off chance someone would pass me the ball; I would, most certainly, be met with a borage of eager feet, swatting and kicking at a chance to gain control of the ball. Missing their intended target however, making contact with every square inch of my leg, from the knee down, and one specifically painful time in the thigh. Damn Seth and his giraffe legs!

Being the last practice before our next game, I was both excited and nervous. Coach Thomas was making us run drills to prepare; running us back and forth, back and forth, yelling through his cupped hands, "Now listen here boys, you better get those knees to your chest when yer tryin' to get dat ball! We ain't got time for you to smell the flowers and watch the clouds rollin' in!" He yells, while gasping for air and trying to keep up with the group. "Pick up the pace! Five passes back and forth! The last player to finish has to sit out the first half of the game against Roland Creek Baptist on Saturday morning! You don't wanna be left on the bench, do ya??" Sounding like Army cadets, we all yelled back; "COACH, NO SIR". "I can't hear y'all!" he yelled back at us. Raising our voices louder for the last pass, "COACH, NO SIR!"

With three short chirps of his whistle, Coach Thomas calls us to come to the center circle to discuss the plan for, in a Christian way, the whooping of Roland Creek Baptist's butt. "Ok so what y'all gonna do is make sure you flank the goal side, keeping their guys off on the Channels. If they reach within goal range you best make sure their Target man ain't sitting there waitin'!" Coach Thomas says while drawing out the sweep diagram on his dry erase clipboard. "Make sure you narrow the gap and push them back on their side; sweep kick if you have to to keep the ball secure and head back to make the goal. Get it close to Jeremiah, he'll be on their goal side in the left channel ready to receive the ball and nail it to the goal." He says as Colby gives a disgruntled "ugh" while rolling his eyes. Lucky for him, his father didn't hear him or he'd have two more drills to do as punishment.

Waving over from the sidelines, Coach Thomas continues, "I'm gonna get Braydon to show you boys what I mean by sweeping the channels and pushing them back to their side." Using his clipboard as a pointer, we follow his arm to see Colby's older brother, Braydon half running, half jogging onto the field. Braydon was home from college for Labor Day and was offering to help out with our practices. He was a stark difference from Colby in height and had a darker olive tone to his skin. Slight dark stubble framed on his jawline, with sandy blonde highlighted hair, up in a messy, wavy bun - bouncing each time his foot made contact with the Carolina Red clay and grass mixed soccer field.

His blue and grey vertical striped shirt looked like he was dipped in wax with each curve and you could see each bulging muscle on display from his broad shoulders down to the small of his waist. I couldn't help but to take in every visual inch of his body in pure astonishment when I realized his running had narrowed his gap to us rather quickly. I was almost drooling at the sight of his mid-thigh length white soccer shorts - so worn down that the stadium lights behind him were making them almost see through. "OMG, I don't think he has any underwear on!" I gasped under my breath. The words falling out of my mouth too quickly to be filtered and I immediately looked around to see if anyone heard me. To my relief; no one had.

Grabbing the ball, kicking it in the air and showing off a bit - he runs to the left goal ready to show us how to run the channels. At this point, I'm still lost on what channels they are talking about. Before soccer, the only channels I knew were on the television and none were playing soccer in our house. The only sport broadcasted in our home, if you can even count it as a sport, was NASCAR. "Ok boys, Colby, Jeremiah, Clay, and Donovan get up and be the defenders" Coach says motioning for us to get up. "Everyone go sit on the bench and watch and learn." He says. "Why me? I have no idea what I'm doing" I huffed to myself, but still ran to join the others.

Standing at the 3 o'clock position of center field, I hear Coach yell, "Ok son, show 'em how it's done." And with that Braydon starts zigzagging with the ball flipping from front to back, spinning around and kicking the ball from left to right and back again. Trying his best to keep us from anticipating his next move as he approached the center field, I vaguely knew that I was supposed to stand guard from the center point up to the goal point - that's when Jeremiah and Colby would take over. Trying to mirror his motions - I hold my ground ready for him to blast past me.

Braydon barreled towards me while expertly maintaining control of the ball. His muscular frame seemed to be making a beeline to the one square foot of grass beneath my feet. Hearing my coach's words in my head, I held my ground, crouching, ready to advance to whichever side he chose. Before I could lean to one side or the other, Braydon's sweaty body slammed into me in full stride. Snapping my head back, his force sent me flying from my position, the impact making me briefly lose consciousness.

I opened my eyes a bit sluggish with a slight ringing in my ears. "OH Crap dad! I'm sorry, I didn't think he would stay there, I thought he was going to move, I'm so sorry. Flabbergasted, Braydon is standing over my dazed body that is now laying flat on the ground. "Is he ok? Did he get knocked out cold? Is he breathing?" As my eyes fully open I can see Braydon and all the other guys bending over me looking down and calling my name. "Let me see, I'm sure he's fine but, boys move on now, let me in there!" Coach says pushing the circled players out of the way to get on the ground to assess my possible injuries.

"Boy, when I told you to not let anyone get by you; you took that literally! That's what we call going above and beyond the call of duty!" Coach says with a chuckle in his voice while pulling my shoulders to put me in a sitting position. Still dazed, I look around to see everyone around me all looking concerned at the sight of me taking a direct hit from a half-ton bulldozer. "Walk him over and sit him on the ground in front of the bench, I don't want him passing out and falling and hitting his head." Coach says as Colby and Jeremiah get under each arm and walk me to the bench.

"Holy crap Van! You didn't let him by, that's for sure!" Jeremiah says in a surprised, yet proud tone. "Yeah! You went right in to get that ball and I think you would have had it too if Bray wasn't running so fast. You did kick the ball out of his control though." Says Colby in the same inflection as Jeremiah. Looking over my shoulder I see Clay running to where Braydon had started his charge to see him bending down and getting the ball to reset the play. "The ball made it all the way to the goal, there's no way I defended AND kill-kicked it to the goal?" I say with disbelief and questioning in my voice. "You sure as hell did and gave me a right nice bruise on my shin to go with it." Says Braydon, surprised that he's now behind me as the guys bend to sit me on the ground. "The way you committed to play like that was on a professional level! You weren't letting me through there without a fight," Braydon says, while rolling his shin guard down to show a freshly made six inch gauge of skin. "OMG! I'm so sorry Braydon, I um…. Really didn't mean to… I mean, I was..." Braydon waved me off, "Nah man, nature of the game!"

My best friend's brother was now standing over me while I leaned my back on the bench, my head started spinning - it was almost too much. This olive skin Adonis telling me I did a great job playing soccer was making me feel light headed and a bit confused. Either that or I had a concussion, I wasn't entirely sure. A huge smile begins to lift the corners of my mouth as I look up and realize that I am now eye level to a familiar pair of almost transparent white shorts. Braydon, still standing in front of me, obviously now talking to someone standing behind me, was within a foot of my actual face, proving that my presumption of him being commando was true. I could see a very defined shadow below his waist line, only about an inch or two from the bottom of the seam on the left side of his mid-thigh length shorts. My mouth unexpectedly fell open and froze. I couldn't gather words or thoughts at that moment. The stadium lights provided the perfect lighting for a full on exposure of my best friend's twenty year old brother's dick and it was on full display, for my eyes to take in. I could tell he was well endowed and was proud of it. Hell, I would be too if I had to tuck that thing in a pair of underwear every day. No wonder he went commando; I doubt it would fit!

He had to know! There is no way you can hide a kickstand that big without underwear, especially wearing white! For what seemed like an hour, in all actuality about thirty seconds - I had a personal one-on-one show and it was stirring a feeling in me that was becoming all too familiar. "Are you ok? Like seriously? Do you need anything?" Says Colby running over while shooing away his older brother. My gaze followed Braydon towards the parking lot where a red SUV pulled up beside the field with a girl around his age driving. "Yes, I'm fine. I'll be ok, I promise. Don't say anything to my mother about this! She will make me go get x-rays and tell everyone about my "Tragic Accident" or "Show of Bravery" in the weekly family newsletter." I said sarcastically, rubbing the back of my neck. There was no actual newsletter, but I swear my mother talks to everyone. If I didn't know any better; she could pick up the phone, hit one number, and be on the phone with all 5 of her sisters and 3 best friends; at the same time! She was seriously the one you didn't want to tell a secret too.

"We don't want that to happen to you! Are you sure you're ok?" Jeremiah says now crouching down beside me. Reassuring them again, I stand up and regain my footing on earth and do a sad but funny dancing jig, side to side, trying to prove that my bearings were still there. "Good, because if you guard like that on Saturday, we definitely will be wiping the field with Roland Creek Baptist!" Colby says, giving me a high-five as he runs back to the now emptied center circle with his father.

"I'm glad you're ok, I was going to ask you if you wanted to come hangout after the game Saturday? Jeremiah says while packing his duffle bag. "I asked my mom about having friends stay the night and she said she's cool with it as long as we don't get too rowdy." he said as he was slinging his bag over his shoulder, "The girls won't bother us because they will be at Seth's house for a sleep over with his sister Renee, and Mary is touring some college with my aunt up in Virginia. So we can just chill and have a good time. You game?" "Sure! Is Colby coming over or anyone else?" I ask, "Nah, I don't think he can. His dad's been on his butt all week. Something about some essays missing from English and a bunch of math homework. I don't think we will have a "Guys" weekend anytime soon." Jeremiah says, while pointing out to the center circle at Colby being made to do pushups under his father's watchful eye.

As parents started arriving to pick up their players - each covered in a mixture of grass stains, dirt and distinct orange splashes from the red mud. I noticed my mom pull up, creeping over to the last spot available on the front row of parking spaces. Running to the driver's side window and motioning for her to roll her window down she flips the interior light on and does just that. "Hey baby! You look like you've been run over by a truck and left for dead!" She says with a giggle in her voice. "He basically was!" Yells Colby from two cars over. "Dude! Shut up!" Snapping back at him, giving the international sign for zip it! "Jeremiah wanted to know if it was ok if I spent the weekend with him at his house? Of course, I'll finish my homework, and do my chores. I'll even help Emmalee do hers and clean my room. and…" Cutting me off, my mother holds up both hands to stop me. "Darling, no need to sell yourself to the devil! I'm ok with you going. Just make sure it's ok with his parents and I'll make sure you have your stuff washed and ready for church when we leave for your game Saturday morning." Surprised by how easy it was to get a "yes" I ran immediately over to Jeremiah and gave him a thumbs up. "She's game, I'll see you Saturday! If you want me to bring anything just let me know." I say to him as his mother was putting his duffle bag in the backseat of their Black Tahoe.

"Hey sweetie!" Ms. Denise cheerfully greets me. "Jeremiah says he wants you to stay over this weekend, Of course, we're ok with it. What's your favorite snack and drink? And I'll make sure you boys are all set for whatever adventures you can think of." "Thank you Ms. Denise, I'm fine with just water and the basic stuff. Nothing fancy. Thank you for letting me come over, I promise to not get in the way." I was laying it on thick because for the duration of the sleepover, she would be the one to dole out praise and/or punishment.

Running back to the passenger side of the van, I jump in as my mother turns the overhead light off. "We're good, mom. Ms. Denise said it was cool. I promise I'll be good." I said while buckling my seat belt. "Oh, I know you will! Because if you're not; I don't care if it's 2AM, I'll come get you and trust me honey, you don't want me showing up in my nightgown, housecoat and curlers." My mother says laughing.

"Mom! You don't even own curlers! Your hair is almost as short as mine!" I said, rolling my eyes. "I'll buy some at the Dollar General just to make sure I look the part. Don't test me because you know I'll do it!" She says motioning as if her hair was in full bee-hive style. "Oh! I know you will mom! Trust me, I don't doubt you would!"

Chapter Nine

"Get on out dar and show 'em how it's done, son!" Catcalls my father from the steel built, half-rusted grandstands that were situated parallel to the perfectly lined #3 Field at the City Rec Center. Rolling my eyes, embarrassed, I run to the center circle and shoulder tap Brody, a short, dumpy team mate, signaling that I was taking his place on the field. Similar to my choice on participation; Brody obviously was being forced to be on the team even though he clearly had no desire. "Hey! Good job bud! I'm here to relieve you," saying while the time-out buzzer ticks closer to zero. "Coach says to head to the bench." "Hallelujah!!" The relief plastered on his face. "These Roland Creek guys are running my butt off!" Galloping back to the bench, Brody leaves me standing in his center position to run out the clock and get this game sealed. Scanning the field, I find the opposing teammate I was tasked with to cover and block; a skinny, taller than usual, dark curly haired guy, around my age, with sport goggles and mix matched shin guards.

He seemed easy enough to keep up with but before the referee blew his starting whistle to end the other team's requested time-out; a warm hand slid down my shoulder. "Hey man! You have been working your butt off for this moment." A familiar voice leans in from behind. He was close enough to my ear that I could feel a warm burst of breath rolling from his lips, directly into my ear drum. It was Jeremiah! "What the heck man!" I say, turning around in surprise. "Dude, you scared me to death!" Dramatically grabbing my chest as he runs past me, holding both thumbs up and yelling back at me. "You got this and trust me, their star kicker busted his knee and all we need to do now is hold them off and get me that ball and I'll handle the rest!" Jeremiah now in his assigned position, five feet to my left; crouching down with his hands on his knees like a bull waiting for the gates to open. Assuming my stance, I crouch down and find my guy - locking into his position and wait for the chaos to begin.

"CHIRP CHIRP CHIRP!!" The high pitched whistle rings off the trees as the referee hands the ball to the opposite team to throw-in to finish the final seconds of the last half of the game. Passing the ball, back and forth, player to player - I stand my ground waiting for "goggles guy" to get close to the center circle where I was stationed.

At the 50 yard mark, Colby intercepts the ball, stealing control and running around to the opposite channel where Jeremiah was propped, waiting for the pass. With a lofted pass, Jeremiah has the ball under his foot. The grandstands erupt in a clatter of cheers and yelling, meant to keep all of us on track. Above all of the parent's voices I hear my mother's insufferable screech, "Van! You betta' keep 'em on their side, don't give up your place. You betta narrow that gap over there" Apparently, my mother became a Soccer Olympic Gold Medalist in the last 3 months of practices and games.

Jeremiah runs a fake and gets around the gathering of Roland Creek players and finds a clear shot. With his bottom lip tucked tight under the tip of his top teeth; he pulls back, and takes his shot. A full force kick sends the ball sailing, two inches above the goalie, lifting the back of the net with its impact and scoring the winning point! Celebration for us was easier than the defeat for the Roland Creek guys. Our teammates from the bench and on the field, created a mosh pit around Jeremiah and Colby. High fives and plenty of jumping around, celebrating our well-earned victory.

Packing the last few empty water bottles in a white trash bag, Coach Thomas makes a quick pass through the bench area. Reminding us for the third time, "We always leave a place better than we found it." "Man, that was a perfect game! I knew I'd get a clear channel with you guys guarding off the other team," Jeremiah says while throwing his duffle bag over his pride-filled shoulders. "Van, you ready to go?" he asked while walking up to me and Colby as we were packing the last of our pads in our bags. Adding an extra pep to my step in excitement, "I sure am, let me just get my stuff from the car and I'll meet you in the parking lot." Slamming his half zipped bag to the dirt, "Seriously! That's totally uncool, guys!" Complains Colby. "Totally unfair!"

"Dude, if you get your school work done and get off restriction; next weekend it's game on at my house! I just got the new Grand Tourismo game ready for us too!" Jeremiah says while walking to meet his parents at their Tahoe.

Ignoring Colby's insistent whining, I meet my parents to trade off my gear for my overnight bag. "Now, you listen and you listen good." My mother says while holding tight to the strap of my bag; unwilling to release her grip until I agree to her terms. "You will be polite, and you will treat their home with respect. If I hear about any rough housing or back-talking at Sunday school in the morning; I promise it'll take Jesus himself to save your hide from having a date with my wooden spoon. Ya hear me?" Irritated but maintaining a respectful tone, I smile wide, "Yes ma'am, I promise!"

Thankfully, the Davis' Tahoe was very spacious with Ms. Denise and Pastor Rich in the front seats. Jeremiah and I had both rows to ourselves in the back. Talking about nothing special we continued out of the parking lot as the excitement started to boil in my gut. Reaching their neighborhood, Pastor Rich slows his speed, unintentionally allowing me time to enjoy the beautiful mansions at the entrance. Reaching their driveway, stopping short of the garage, Jeremiah and I jump out and head into the house through the now open garage door. Stopping at the doorway to disarm the house's ear-piercing ADT alarm, Jeremiah enters the code and the beeping stops. Dropping his soccer bag and cleats, he grabs two Gatorades from the fridge and yells back at his parents, "We'll be downstairs, let us know when dinner is ready. Is that ok mom?" Bending to pick up the discarded soccer gear now an obstacle in the doorway, Ms. Denise replies, "Honey, we really don't have anything planned, so you boys fend for yourselves tonight - make a sandwich or something and Donovan," "Yes Ma'am?" I say quickly, almost interruptive, flashing back to my mother's lecture, "You treat our home like your own. If you want something, don't ask, just grab it." She says while filling a glass with ice from the freezer. "I greatly appreciate it Ms. Denise, thank you so much for letting me stay." I say, while trying to catch up with Jeremiah, who is now at the bottom of the stairs.

Shutting the door behind me, I realize that we have the entire basement to ourselves for a true guy's weekend. Thrilled to be out of my small bedroom of solitude and living the life of space and luxury with my best friend for a night. I was sure to have my fill of junk food and video games. The excitement was almost too much. Following Jeremiah to his room, setting my stuff in the far corner of the room, around the large dresser mirror. I ask, "Ok if I put my stuff here?", looking to make sure he was cool with it. Jeremiah reaches to open a drawer, grabbing a pair of gym shorts and a tee shirt. "Yeah man! Mi casa es sus casa!" he says while pulling his dirt and grass stained jersey over his head.

Gazing at his full upper body, turning to his bathroom door, he pulled his pants and underwear down in one swift motion - exposing a stark white, slim, dimpled, firm ass - and it was less than five feet from me. I couldn't believe my eyes as my heartbeat increased and there was a thundering pounding in my chest. Shyly, I grab my bag; acting as if I'm searching for something in case he turns to see my drooling. "First shower!" He calls out while walking in the bathroom completely naked, turns the water on and starts his shower. Away from his direct sight, my head begins to feel dizzy. Collapsing on the foot of his bed, I try to wrap my head around what just happened. I had seen almost all of him, and weirdly, he seemed very comfortable in holding nothing back. That confidence gave me more of that unsettling, yet increasingly familiar feeling in my gut.

It felt like an eternity for Jeremiah to finish his shower, as I laid waiting on his bed, staring at the ceiling fan. Hearing the water turn off, I find my bag, not to ignore him, but to find something to wear after my turn in the shower. While I was digging out my toiletry bag, Jeremiah emerged, now only draped in a white and blue striped towel. Still a little wet, Jeremiah walked into the room, motioning that I was next. Grabbing my things, careful to hold them in front of my waist; trying to be nonchalant at hiding my strong arousal. Walking past him, trying to not notice his glistening body, I accidentally grazed his shoulder as the wetness of his clean body leaves a smudge on my jersey. In the bathroom, I quickly undressed and started my shower. Allowing the water to pelt my face in an attempt to cleanse my thoughts from going anywhere they shouldn't be.

After a quick shower, I dry myself completely, and get dressed in blue nylon basketball shorts and a grey American Eagle t shirt. Walking through the steam filled doorway to his room I find him sitting on the bed, flipping through what looked to be a sports magazine, while chugging an orange sports drink. "So, what do you want to do man?" Saying while standing up from the bed. "We can do whatever!" "Doesn't matter to me, I'm game for anything." I say, while putting my dirty clothes in a pile next to my stuff in my corner of his room. "I don't mind just watching TV or playing Grand Tourismo, it's totally your call."

Jeremiah starts looking side to side, as if someone could be eavesdropping in the room, "Well, we could have some fun, but you have to promise no one can know!" Once he was confident in us being the only ones around he said, "I got a magazine from Colby last week, and when I tell you.…..It's….well….you'll just have to see." He says, lifting the front corner of the mattress to dig out his hidden gift.

Pulling out another magazine, he sits down near the headboard and opens it while telling me to sit down next to him to see. I was shocked! It was a "DIRTY" magazine! I'd never seen one in person, and now with me holding the left side of the page, my sheer nerves took over at the thought of his parents coming down the stairs, catching us doing the unholiest of things under their roof. I had no doubt that if caught, I would get my ass handed to me by way of a wooden spoon and an angrily embarrassed mother.

"Don't worry, if they open the door, we will have plenty of time to stash it before they make it to my room and trust me, I've had this thing out every day since I got it." His voice is full of confidence as he opens to the first page. "Colby swiped it from his dad's garage three weeks ago. And when he was done with it, he gave it to me. Coach Thomas apparently has stacks of them behind his workout equipment." He continues while turning through the pages. I couldn't find a single word to say, my jaw frozen at what my eyes were seeing - excessive amounts of exposed breasts and women in various states of undress on each and every page.

Reaching the centerfold, Jeremiah turns the magazine, letting the page's accordion fold out, showing a half poster sized picture of a petite brunette woman with a muscular bald man holding her from the side. "This has guys in it too!" I say, a little loudly at the surprise of seeing muscles on the page. A stark difference to the curves of the women. "Well yes man! It has guys and girls. But if you look at the inside back cover; it has pictures with just guys! It's totally unreal!" Jeremiah says while taking control of the pages again, flipping through to the back cover.

"GAY" in bold print at the top of the page - a full page of men, each with different body types.

***

*Some muscular, some slimmer builds, all in exaggerated acrobatic-like positions with other men! Like the previous pages, the slim guys looked to be in the same positions as the women. "Wooohhh! I didn't even know that was a thing!" I exclaimed. "What are they doing?" I ask while pointing at an enlarged picture at the center of a guy leaning over the hood of a shiny red mustang. He was tattooed, very muscular, and completely naked, as a skinnier man kneels in front of him with his head buried in the guy's lap.

"Van, are you sayin' you don't know what he's doing?" A smirky toned Jeremiah says, looking up to me from the magazine. "He's …. Well…how do you say? He's sucking him, well his….you know!" My eyes lock back to what was being illustrated right in front of my eyes in full colored print. My face grimaces, confused, I ask, "Why would someone do that? How could that even feel good?" looking over at Jeremiah, hoping for clarification.

Standing to adjust himself, then sitting back down, he quickly returns to the same page, "Well, I don't know what it feels like but by the look on his face, it looks like it feels awesome." He says while looking over at me. "I wonder if that's what sex is like?" as if I knew more on that subject than he did. "Heck, I have no clue! I exclaim, while shaking my head. "I've never had anyone touch my junk except when Dr. Kennedy made me do the 'turn and cough' thing for my physical." I notice Jeremiah adjusting himself again, this time without standing up. "I wouldn't know either, but I bet it feels good. I mean, Daphne put her hand on my lap at The Wilderness Church Camp this past summer but only for a second before the counselor came around the building." He says with a smile beaming ear to ear.

Daphne was one of the large flock of girls in our youth group, a year older than us and well over-developed. Anyone with eyes could tell she was head-over-heels for Jeremiah and would attach herself to his hip if given the chance. "You dawg! You never said anything about that" landing a strong punch to his left shoulder "Daphne was touching you? What the hell man! Did it feel good?" I asked. "Well…..it felt…um…. like this!" Jeremiah says as he placed his opened palm square in the middle of my crotch!

"Um….what are you doin?" Confused, I ask as my voice begins to shake. "You wanted to know, and we're friends so it's not like it's crazy or weird." Jeremiah reassures me, proving it wasn't a dream and I wasn't doing anything actually wrong. Closing the magazine and laying on his pillow, he grabs my hand and places it on his shorts on the same spot he was now taking up on mine. I feel that he is already at full mast, causing my hand to quiver, unsure of what to do.

Jeremiah instructs me, "When Daphne had her hand on my lap, she was moving her hand around like this," mimicking her motions, adding friction to my already growing manhood under two very thin barriers of fabric. Not knowing what to do, I followed his lead, creating the same motion and pressure that he was creating for me. Before long, we were rubbing each other vigorously. At one point, I was concerned a fire would spark between the friction of the nylon and skin, causing the fabric of my shorts to overly heat and burst into flames. "Yeah, that does feel really good!" Closing my eyes, allowing them to roll to the back of my head. "Yeah! I told you!" Jeremiah says while adding a bit more downward push to each rub he was giving my now fully engorged package. "Had that counselor not come around the corner; I don't know if I would have stopped her."

Picking up the magazine, leaving my dick feeling awkwardly lonely at his absence; he flips back to the back page again. Pointing at the close up picture with the guy on the car hood, he questions, "The only thing I have been curious about is this!" Jeremiah slows his words in focus as he points to the guy's manhood half in the mouth of a blonde haired, tan mechanic that I'm assuming is fixing this lucky man's car. Bewildered, barely able to find my voice, I ask, "What do you mean? How does it feel to lick a guy's dick?"

At that moment, I wondered if this was all a trick or if this was actually happening. "Yeah man! I mean, I'm not like these guys or anything but I'm just curious what it feels like. Closing the magazine, narrowing his eyes to catch my attentive gaze. "Guys seem to really like it, and the girls too. Like….I don't know man, I know it's weird, but I don't think it's wrong to experiment sometimes. Just so if a girl wants to try something, I know what to expect and not be surprised or freaked out." Standing to put the magazine back under his mattress, Jeremiah sits down, allowing our thighs to touch. Leaning into the heat of my body, releasing whatever apprehensions I had about it being a trick.

Still on his bed, Jeremiah leans over and whispers in my ear. "If you do it to me, I'll do it to you." His voice begging in his urges, "I don't trust anyone else to try this with and I know you're cool with it, so why not try? If it's not cool, just say so and I'll never bring it up again, but I'm dying to see." My eyes moved to the subtle motion of him rubbing himself through his shorts, his eyes were locked with mine. I couldn't hide the erupting curiosity bubbling inside my gut as I nod my head and muster a faint, "Ok....only if you don't tell anyone and you have to promise that If I do it to you, you do it to me." I say while looking for an affirmative answer or if I was going to be shut down by fear. "And I swear, no one better find out about this, Jer! I mean it!" He agrees as he stands, pulling the waistband of his Adidas shorts under his balls, cupping his fully hard cock while releasing an eager, "Deal!"

I positioned myself down on the rough carpet, pushing my body between his opened knees, not fully prepared for the experience. Unsure, I take his fully engorged manhood in my left hand, wrapping my fingers around the shaft, giving it a grip similar to how I would hold my own. My touch released a long sigh from Jeremiah, now slowly laying flat on the bed with his legs off the side. In this position, his tool was standing at full attention, inches from my face. His eyes closed shut and with both hands behind his head. Looking up at his face, his heart was beating a mile a minute as my attention to his tool was careening him over the edge. His cock was bigger than mine and shaped differently too. I swear it looked bigger than Braydon's in his see-through shorts at practice the other night. Jeremiah's pink, almost purple head curved downward, weighing heavy towards his balls making a perfectly over-pronounced "C" shape.

"Wow, yours is shaped different than mine. It's hella thick Jer!" Comparing it to my wrist to show him in contrast. Propping up on both elbows, Jeremiah staring down at me, showing his frustration on my delayed start. "Is this a physical or are you going to do it or not?" Without more direction, I close my eyes, hold my breath and go for it. Wrapping my lips around my teeth, I allow the head of his knob to pass through my lips and onto my tongue, letting the head linger into the voids of my mouth. Adjusting my jaw to open more, and unbeknownst to me at the time, giving me a taste of something that catapulted into a need of more.

While servicing my friend's explorations, I was slowly coming to grips with the feelings I've had over the last few months. I was beginning to set in stone what the unknowns had been. "Is this what I've been feeling?" I thought to myself, with his dick half in my mouth. Still not moving, staying in place, trying to get familiarized with the silky feel on my lips. "Am I what that page says, 'GAY' or is this normal for buddies to do with each other?" I didn't have time to think further before Jeremiah's hands found the back of my head, slowly pushing me down farther. Granting him control, I let him pull me down farther only to be met with a strong urge to gag.

Returning to the top of his dick, clearing my throat, I go back for another try. This time, a salty taste lingered as I pulled up and down on his slippery wet cock. His penis was releasing a clear liquid in response to my warm mouth. In that moment, I tried not to think, living in the moment and savoring what Jeremiah was giving me. Following his lead, I increase my pace going up and down his hard shaft - with his hands on the back of my head, the veins pulsating with each pass of my lips. Finding a rhythm, I let the insecurities leave my body as if I was floating above both of us, watching from the ceiling. I kept reminding myself to not go so deep where I would gag because I didn't want to have to start all over again.

I was in pure ecstasy and couldn't tell you why or how to stop it. But did I want to stop it? I honestly didn't think I did! I wanted this, I wanted to experience what those pictures were showing. Unsure, I wondered if I was doing it right? Flashing in my mind to the pictures in the magazines, trying to remember what the girls and guys were doing. By the sounds coming from Jeremiah, I would say yes, I was doing a satisfactory job. Looking down at my own abandoned manhood, a wet spot forming on the front of my pants, my body was responding to pleasure even though my turn had yet to come, simply by what Jeremiah was experiencing and how his body was responding to my vigorous work. **

***

I felt more connected to him than anyone else, and if this is what I was, then I needed to have a first time. I never felt a connection to anyone like I was now having with Jeremiah. During this exploration, his place as "Best Friend" was cemented in my mind. I wanted to be in this moment with my best friend, both of us eager to explore where our bodies could lead us. Unwrapping and discovering the feelings that had been brewing deep inside me with someone I now fully trusted. I had faith in him to hold the secrets of what we had done from getting out to anyone else. Since we took the plunge together, my first sexual secrets would forever be in his safekeeping. And that was Jeremiah - he would forever be crowned - my first.

Chapter Ten

My emotion and trust intertwined easily but was shrouded in naivety. The strong emotions of not knowing what I was feeling or why, mixed with trying to trust Jeremiah in leading this sexual exploration of each other had shown me just how fragile I was.

I was enjoying the exploration process, but before I could relish in my feelings of wonder and accomplishment - it ended; leaving me with more yearning and desire. What happened with Jeremiah that night didn't give me a choice of a stopping-place. It just happened; leaving me vulnerable and scared.

How could I not have feelings after that night? I thought while I was daydreaming in my third period Chemistry class, not paying any attention to Mr. Long's lesson on Polyatomic Ions. Two months had come and gone with little change to my boring daily existence. With the last game on the horizon, I knew the final nail in the coffin for soccer would be the awards banquet. An over excited celebration: mostly for the MVPs and a collection of parents who take youth sports way too seriously. You know, those parents who think their little "Johnny" is the next all-star player, proudly displaying every plastic metallic trophy and shiny satin gilded ribbon on their fireplace. If I did win any of the awards, it would end up lost in a sea of junk on the shelves in my bedroom; later to be discarded as wasteful memorabilia with no meaningful attachments.

We weren't going to the playoffs and I didn't care either way. The district star team, Drayton Baptist, swept every game with a win while we lost four of our eleven games. It was safe to say, my cleats would be in my closet before the turkey was on the table for Thanksgiving. I couldn't be more ready for this break. Having to participate in all the youth events at our church, with practices every Thursday, and a game every Saturday morning; had brought my mind and body to full on exhaustion.

"MR. SHELTON!" Mr. Long yells while throwing a red dry erase marker - close enough to get my attention but far enough not to actually hit me. "Mr. Shelton, If you are going to zone out while in my class; at least lay your head down on your desk" trailing off mid-sentence, my teacher scans over the classroom. "Like Mr. Brunson over there." Mr. Long says with his jaw clenched in a louder tone, hurling a blue marker across the classroom at Brad Brunson, forcing him to snap up from his post-lunch slumber. I swear, Mr. Long must have an army supply of attention missiles in his desk, never missing a chance to use them on anything but the white board.

"Mr. Shelton, now that I have your attention - What is the correct molecular formula for phosphoric acid?" Looking lost and void of an answer, I shamefully admit, "I have no clue!" "Mr. Long, If I may," interrupting as usual, the know-it-all red head in the front of every class, Monica Santos blurts out, "The correct answer is H_3PO_4 Mr. Long!" Taking the attention away from me, my teacher smiles while praising Monica for paying attention but returns to drilling other classmates on various questions for the final next week.

I didn't care about molecules or elements; my mind was engulfed with the unfinished emotions of the last few months. I couldn't stop thinking about that September night with Jeremiah - replaying the things I had done and saw, like it was a movie on never-ending repeat, in my head, and I couldn't find the remote to turn it off.

The experience that night lasted barely five minutes before Jeremiah abruptly stopped me, satisfied in his own curiosity and wanting nothing more. Almost as frustrating as being stopped mid-experience, Jeremiah didn't follow through with his end of the deal. My curiosity wasn't fulfilled, I didn't get the same experience that he had. When Jeremiah wanted to stop, I had no choice but to comply. We both got dressed, went to the game room and acted like nothing happened. Jeremiah was kind enough to bring me two blankets from the closet under the stairs and a pillow from his bed. My dream of waking in the morning next to my personal Adonis began running farther away from my actual reality.

Cuddling his pillow, I could smell the lingering scent of his cologne, burying my head, trying to recapture the moments before being told to stop. Aimlessly, we watch reruns of The Fresh Prince, not saying a word about what happened in his room. Feeling guilty at the thought of God, up in heaven using his golden eraser to remove me from the acceptance list for the Pearly Gates. I know I lost my place in heaven. All because of some stupid teenage urges that couldn't be controlled.

I could have just said "No". Either way, I would have been left feeling the same way - blue balled and guilt-ridden! Adjusting my package, still raging with unreleased testosterone, a feeling rolls from my tightened balls up to my chest. The thudding sound playing in my chest was drowning out the audience's laughter, as my brain continued to turn against me. I was over the constant tug-o-war between my heart and brain. Something had to give, I had to admit to myself what I was, deal with the consequences, and acknowledge the permanent disconnection from my faith - but I couldn't do that. I couldn't walk away from what I had known my entire life. I couldn't walk away from the one person that was there for me when no one else was, turning my back on God couldn't be the only option.

Before shutting the lights off to the game room, Jeremiah hesitated at the stairway, just past the sectional. With his back to me, looking down the short hall to his room, in a subdued monotone voice, he breaks the silence, "You know, that was fun - I don't think we need to do that again. But.... are we cool?" Still not looking back but looking at the ground, I assume from the shame building inside him, on what had just transpired. "Man, of course we are. You are my best friend and I'm ok, if you are ok."

I was obviously lying through my teeth and wanted to do it again or at the very least, have his mouth on my now deflating prick that was sticking to the inside of my shorts. Jeremiah sluggishly started towards his room, one foot in front of the other, slowly picking up his stride as he climbed into his bed, and turned off his bedside lamp. The basement was pitch black, with no sound coming from anywhere. I could hear the hum from the refrigerator upstairs, mocking me, at the emptiness I felt in the room. Struggling to find a comfortable position on the long side of the sectional, I kept beating myself up for what I had done. I doubt I'll have a chance like that again and most likely, it wouldn't be with him.

Abruptly awakened from my personal hell, the class change bell bounces off the science lab walls, ringing three times to signal the last class of the day and then its home for the weekend. Even though it was almost quitting time on Friday, I had nothing exciting happening. Not even the soccer match tomorrow morning; It was a technicality game, it didn't have any purpose. We didn't have to win; our place in the tournament bracket would still be the same - nowhere near first, second, or even third place. The game would be followed by the unnecessary award's ceremony - and then church on Sunday and that's it - no more soccer practice nor faking excitement for a team sport that had been shoved down my throat by my parents.

Chapter Eleven

Self hatred and doubt can ruin a person's mental health. The weight of such a huge secret can transform a normal person into a shell of what they once were. The standards one place on their own shoulders can be heavier than the obligations surrounding them, causing an overwhelming sense of guilt. The guilt being the catalyst to the spiraling effects on the brain, sending a person over the edge, unable to escape the dance between reality and what their brains are telling them would or has happened.

I didn't necessarily hate myself for the acts I had done, but rather, hated myself for acting on my urges. It pulled me even farther from what was expected of me by my family and the church. It was understood that being a good Christian teen was someone who followed the teachings of Christ to the letter. You weren't allowed to rock the boat and explore anything outside of the norms. My life choices weren't up to me but were determined by the church's belief of following the literal words of the Bible. My family drilled into my head that staying pure in my thoughts was just as important as having pure actions. Even though my impure thoughts belonged to me, it caused a guilt within me that would send me to my knees, begging God for forgiveness. I was expected to find a good Christian girl, marry her, then have a family. Continuing the long tradition of maintaining the perfect facade while pushing any unholy desires away.

I knew, based on the teachings of the Bible, that I was backsliding from my faith, allowing my desires to overrun the rules of the church. The anger I felt toward myself wasn't of my own conviction. It was the obligations placed on what I was expected to be in the eyes of my church and family. I couldn't let anyone know what I had done, I would never live it down.

Not only did I have premarital relations with another person; it was a same-sex act. But was it so bad? Seeing as though I was only following directions, and not receiving the actual sexual act on my own body. Neither of us reached over the edge with an orgasm, so would it even be considered a sexual act? Does that mean my purity was left intact? The worries bounced back and forth between my brain and my heart, in an endless repetition, with no comfort in sight.

My body went into autopilot as I walked to my next class on the other side of the building. I couldn't stop thinking about Jeremiah and our five-minute failure and the fact that he acted like nothing even happened. He was still the team leader of "The Guys." He was still charming as ever and full of horrible jokes. Nonetheless, he acted as if nothing was different and kept insisting I hang out with everyone after each service. But how could he go on like nothing happened? My frame was heavy with worry as I walked through the red doors of the library for fourth period, my easy credit class needed for the year. I spent the rest of my school day reading books and keeping people from hanging out between the shelves while trying to skip class.

Unable to shake the worry from my gut, I sat behind the computer desk and opened my chemistry textbook, trying to direct my brain to something productive. It wasn't working, it was sending me straight back to that bottomless well of worry and self hatred. Had I been that bad at it? Did he not like how I was sucking him? Did he not realize how difficult it was to do that for him? He had discarded me, pushed me away, as if my feelings didn't matter. My mind kept falling down that well of self loathing as my gaze to nothingness peered over my textbook at the empty library wall. All I wanted was for the final bell to sound, releasing me from my state funded educational prison.

"Hey Van! What's on your mind?" announced a familiar voice, as he dropped three books on Julius Caesar, inches from face, snapping me back into reality. In my self-loathing coma, I missed Colby signing in at the front door, and wandering about the dusty book racks for his selections. Looking at the books, I knew Colby wasn't the intellectual type and I doubted he wanted these books for pleasure. I assumed they were for a makeup project, in hopes of bringing up his English grade to barely passing while keeping his parents off his ass. "Dude! Seriously! What the hell has been going on? Repeating himself, he snaps his fingers inches from my nose, "You're always deep in thought lately, so spill it …now!" Not wavering from his question, he stood, arms crossed, looking for the reason for my disconnection from reality.

Looking square into my eyes, burning his concentrated stare through the back of my skull, Colby waited patiently for a response that wasn't going to happen. I couldn't say anything about what happened with Jeremiah. Regardless of Jeremiah not keeping up his end of the deal, I would keep my promise of discretion. And even if I wanted to talk about it there was no way to verbalize the tornado of emotions that had been enveloping me since summer. Thinking fast, I blurt out, "I'm flunking chemistry - my parents are going to kill me." Deliberately lying, since I knew I had a solid B in the subject and didn't even need to do well on the final exam to pass the class.

"Dude! I know the feeling!" Colby's tense stance relaxed, relieved that someone was struggling like himself. "Mr. Giovanni is making me do a report on this Caesar guy just to get my English grade to a 71. He's some kind of king or something and honestly, I could care less. I really don't want to repeat English 10, I would lose the little bit of freedom I have with my parents. Being stuck at home with my brother and sister all break is not my idea of a good time." Undoubtedly overwhelmed, Colby pulls his hand down the front of his face, revealing his own misery. "Luckily, he's giving me until the end of this term to finish it so, this weekend I think I can talk mom and dad into having you guys over." Excitement fills his voice, as the need of his project and a passing grade in English takes a backseat to the possibility of one last hoorah before the seriousness of his grades were discovered by his parents.

"Do you think your parents would let you spend the night or do you think you will be grounded for flunking?" He asks, while a small half smile paints across his face. Tapping his pencil on the desk, he impatiently awaits my response, "I'm not sure bud, I'll ask and see, but don't get your hopes up." I say while standing up to scan the barcodes on each book, checking them out properly under his name in the computer system and getting him out of my face.

"I'll ask my mom to call you and Jeremiah's mom." He says, grabbing his checked out books and putting them all in his backpack. Hearing Jeremiah's name made me freeze, locking my sight on the computer screen, unable to stop the replay from happening again in my head. "Seriously! Donovan!!" Raising his voice, Colby now caught the attention of Mrs. Brown, the middle-aged Librarian, who was directly behind the checkout desk, tucked away in her office. Her overly patterned flowery blouse and high-pinned salt and pepper messy bun shaking as she darted her head out from the office door, giving a pinched yet forceful "SHHH-HHH!" causing Colby to step back.

Closing the distance while trying to whisper, Colby pushes again for me to divulge my deepest secret. "Whatever else is going on - you can tell me. I won't tell anyone; you can trust me." A soothing and trusting tone rolls in his voice, "Let's try this one more time, what in the actual hell is going on?"

Holding my ground, I let another white lie fly from my tight pressed lips, in hopes of shutting him up. My loyalty was causing a continual snowball effect of lies and deceit, distancing me from what I knew to be right and wrong. "I think that's a good idea, I haven't been out of the house for the past few months- ever since my last report card." I changed the subject to the sleepover at his house, in hopes of distracting him from my emotional drama. "My mother was pissed with my grades, so most of my time has been spent studying flash cards and rewriting notes." Another lie, "But I'm sure she'll say yes because of the awards ceremony being a special occasion and all." Standing up to walk to the front of the desk; hoping to put an end to the insufferable questioning. "Awesome! I'll call you when I get home!" Colby says in an accomplished tone as he heads out the side door to the math hall. "Make sure to pack a sleeping bag - Braydon will be home, his room is off limits and I doubt you will want to sleep on our lumpy couch." Before I could answer, the door shut with him on the other side, quickly disappearing into the empty hallway, leaving me to return to my post at the front desk.

The quiet hum of the empty library allowed the tormenting thoughts that were paused in my mind to return. Now I had the added stress of spending the night at Colby's for the first time to add to my personal hell. What will happen if my dick decides to be disloyal and gets hard at the sight of all the guys with their shirts off? Let's be honest, I'm not going to attack every guy that shows a bit of skin, but teenage hormones have their own schedule - I never know when a surprise boner will pop up. And frankly, I didn't want it to be anywhere near Jeremiah or anyone from the church if that happened. If I had to come to terms with what was going on then I knew I had to stop connecting my feelings with anyone associated with the church. It was too difficult to deal with God and my own desecration without getting physically attached to my closest friends.

Returning to my isolation, I was too ashamed to admit that I had actually liked what Jeremiah was showing me that day. I enjoyed what I was doing to him. I had to figure out how to make desire take a backseat to my religious obligations. I couldn't let my sexual yearning turn me farther away from what had been drilled into my head as morally and religiously right. I couldn't be one of those guys in the magazine under Jeremiah's bed, in all those sexual positions. Submitting to another man's needs by being his sexual toy and disgracing God and my family while selfishly fulfilling this unhealthy desire. I knew I had to fight it and get over these sensations quickly. The thoughts became unmanageable as goosebumps raced up my arms.

The thought of anyone finding out made my blood run cold and my body involuntarily shake. I just couldn't live in this hell anymore. I had to move on and forget about Jeremiah and the whole experience. I bet he had already forgotten about it and only saw me as a friend; not the person who had been pumping my mouth up and down his engorged veiny shaft. Thankfully, my self-hatred was interrupted by the closing announcements that came on over the intercom. Not paying any attention to what the principal was saying, I gathered my books and headed out the door to the busy hallway.

I didn't want to go to Colby's, but I figured that I would oblige him and just stick to myself for the night. I doubt Jeremiah would say anything to "The Guys" or that he would even admit to our experimenting, but a small part of me wondered if he had the same thoughts playing hell in his mind. Maybe it was fear that caused him to abruptly end everything. "That could make sense and answer a lot of questions, but I am probably wrong." I said under my breath as I slammed my locker door shut, making sure to latch the combination lock before turning into the hoards of students navigating to the pickup lines out in front of the school. If I'm wrong - I'm wrong. No matter what, I had to find out, and this weekend could be my only chance to confront him. Whatever I decided to do, I knew I had to be careful that no one was around when I did.

    I definitely wanted to keep our secret from "The Guys." If they found out, the entire youth group would end up marching us up to the altar, laying hands and praying over us both in classic Baptist dramatics. This would happen right before both of our parents shipped us off to a far-away place to "pray the gay away," in an attempt to rid us of these sinful homosexual demons causing our leap from faith. My heart began to race as sweat ran down my back just as my mother's minivan inched closer around the pickup circle. She was eighth in line from the front car, waiting for everyone to load up their books and clear a path. Pushing past everyone patiently waiting, I walked off the sidewalk to the grass and met her as she stopped the minivan. I climbed in the passenger seat, snapped my seatbelt and closed my eyes, relieved to finally be on my way home. Without greeting my mother, I sat and collected my thoughts as she pulled onto the main highway. As soon as we started driving she immediately started talking about Colby's mom, Ms. Patty, calling her earlier in the day about Colby's sleepover. Letting out a long sigh, I opened my eyes, giving my mother an exhausted, "Ok" as she flashed a big grin confirming her approval and excitement of me spending another night with "The Guys."

Chapter Twelve

"Mom! Do you know where my sleeping bag is?" I yell while digging in the hall closet, frantically engulfed by unfolded bed linens and used shopping bags. Pulling my head out of the doorway to get my mother's attention in the kitchen, I yell louder, "MOM!" Obviously very perturbed at my erratic screaming, I see her leaning from the kitchen at the opposite end of the hallway, pointing a black slotted spoon in my direction, "Boy! If you don't stop screamin' and yellin' at me," she threatens, "It's not my job to keep up with your stuff!" Elevating her voice I hear her yell for my sister, "Emm!" Promptly opening her bedroom door, Emmalee steps into the hallway, looking down at me, ass up in the family closet, rolling her eyes in frustration. "Yes ma'am?" She replied while tossing my red sleeping bag, half unrolled out of her bedroom door. Before my mom could ask Emmalee about my sleeping bag, I yelled back to the kitchen, "Mom, I found it! Emm had it!" Looking back at my sister in irritation at her borrowing my things without asking. "It better not smell like crappy Bath and Body Works or have glitter in it!" I say while trying to dig my way out from the avalanche of family junk. Saying nothing, my sister closes her bedroom door and returns to her own isolation, while ignoring my empty threats.

Colby's mom coordinated with all of our parents to have everyone dropped off after the awards ceremony. Sunday morning we would take two cars to church, making sure everyone was bright and early to Sunday school. My mother relayed the future plans to me while busying herself in the kitchen. Working on her contribution to the awards ceremony banquet, she bounced between cookbooks and the pantry gathering the needed ingredients for the pots on the stove. "Hallelujah!" I thought to myself when I realized she was making potato salad and baked macaroni and cheese. Thankfully, she wasn't trying yet another gelatin surprise for this church function. I wondered if she got the hint since no one touched the last one she brought to the Baker's Baby shower last month. Who wants to eat a blue colored jiggly ring filled with blue tinted pineapple and fruit cocktail? It was a total epic fail, but since they were having a boy, she felt she had to make it blue. This only succeeded in making the suspended jello dessert look like the blue ring on a toilet bowl.

After freezing my ass off the entire game, the last point was ironically scored by Brody. He magically found a hole in the opposing team's defense and nailed a straight-line kick twenty yards back, right into the net. Soaring over the three guys jumping to try and block his efforts you could see the surprise on his face. The same look of surprise was on all of our teammates' faces. Brody had really gotten the hang of the sport over the past few months and for the first time - was the true MVP. He was grinning so big that I thought his head was going to split in two. He ran to the center circle where all of our teammates were celebrating and waiting to congratulate his perfect shot. The final score was 16-2, we earned this landslide victory and deserved to celebrate.

"We slaughtered our opponents by working as a team and having a darn good offense," says Coach Thomas, while high-fiving each player and shaking hands with the parents. "Remember to meet back at the church gym around 5pm this evening. Go home and get ready to celebrate all of the hard work you all put in this season. You guys earned it no matter what!" Using his hands like a makeshift bullhorn, ensuring his instructions were heard by everyone. "Don't forget to dress nice! We will be taking a team picture at the ceremony, so look your best." He says as he dismisses us to our parents, hurrying us along to get ready for a night of recognition and awards.

Wearing my Sunday's best khakis with a blue and white button up plaid shirt and brown suede jacket, I walk in the gym holding a green Tupperware bowl full of what smelled like a giant fart. I scanned the room to see if any of "the guys" had shown up yet, nope, I was first to arrive. A group of team parents were scrambling in the gymnasium, putting the finishing touches on the stage and potluck area as I followed my mother to the buffet table to drop off the food she made. "Hey Patty, where ya want me to put these?" My mother asks while getting the attention of Colby's mother. Ms. Patty was a sweet lady, around the same age as my mother but taller with longer hair. Ms. Patty's curls bounced with every step around the table, grabbing the bowls, she placed them in the perfect place in the middle of the buffet line. "Millie, this looks amazing! I doubt you'll have any leftovers after these boys tear into it." Sharing a laugh while removing the lid to the potato salad, releasing a waft of putrid smell. She and my mother leave me at the end of the table, as they leave, my mother looks back at me, remembering she hadn't arrived alone. "Honey, go find us a good seat; Your father will be here in a bit, he has to drop your sister off at Aunt Leslie's and Uncle David's." My mother was preoccupied with repositioning various platters, ensuring each space on each table was adequately used. Finding a group of chairs in the center row, I put my jacket on the back of a chair, signaling the international sign for, "this seat is taken."

The stage was set up with the clear acrylic podium, perfectly centered with glistening gold plated trophies on tables at either end. Letting out a long sigh, I realized that this ceremony would take longer than I thought. Each one of the trophies signified a player having to come up, shake hands, turn and smile for a picture and then sit back down before the next player could be called. We were going to be here until Sunday school tomorrow if they didn't start soon and we needed to get this show on the road.

Hearing the back main doors clank shut, I turn around to see Pastor Rich and Ms. Denise walk-in carrying several foil pans of food. Like the parting of the Red Sea, they split in opposite directions and place the pans on either end of the buffet tables, just as Jeremiah emerges through the door, empty handed. The color rushed from my face at the sight of Jeremiah, who had Daphne with him, leaning on his arm, grinning like a Cheshire Cat. "What the hell?" I thought to myself, turning my attention back to our empty table.

Apparently, my face said everything that my mouth couldn't because Jeremiah approached me with a half tilted smile, "Hey Van, you know Daphne." Shyly he says while pulling her over to the table where I was now sitting. "Yeah, she wanted to come and I thought it would be cool for her to hang out with all of us," he said while pulling out the chair directly across from me, like a true gentleman, allowing Daphne to sit. The distinct sound of the backdoor opening changed my focus from the puppy love display forced on me. "The Guys" were coming through the set of doors opposite the stage, seeing my chance to escape, I stood and went to get them. Jeremiah follows in tow. Turning to Jeremiah, I playfully punch him in the shoulder, "Dude, what in the world? No one told me that we needed to bring a date to this?" I say half joking. Laughing, Jeremiah says while rubbing his now stinging shoulder, "Ah man! That hurt! Don't be mad at me, she wanted to come, I didn't see a problem - and since she's my girlfriend, I figured why not."

His words hit me like a bullet. "Girlfriend?" I ask with a tremble in my voice, hoping that I had heard wrong. Blushing, Jeremiah stares at his feet while replying, not looking up to see my face. "Ah yeah, we've kinda been dating for a few weeks now. Since she was gone most of the summer, she didn't get to see us play so she wanted to make sure she was here for this." As quick as the first bullet hit my chest, it was followed by yet another, larger bullet; he said summer. That means, he was talking with her when I spent the night at his house, the night of our exploration, well, more-so, his exploration. Feeling like a fool, I leave Jeremiah to greet the guys, I retreat, turning from the guys, and return to my seat, directly across from the girl that, for some reason, I was now jealous of.

Seeing her lean into him as the ceremony started made my stomach turn. He had his arm on her shoulder, nestling her close, yet not close enough that his parents would be concerned about their public display of affection. Why was I overrun with all of these jealous feelings? My brain started spinning out of control, taking my heart down with it, as each question of my pure existence played war in my head. "Was I in love with Jeremiah?" I thought, while playing with the last cold bites of Baked Macaroni and cheese on my styrofoam plate - moving it from side to side, unable to put it in my mouth.

"Why did this hit me so hard, it wasn't like Jeremiah belonged to me." Confused, I looked up from my plate only to see Jeremiah and Daphne watching the Coach who was behind the podium. Under my breath I whisper, "I wish I was in her shoes." I wanted to be leaning in close to him, his arm around me, feeling secure and safe in his muscular arms. Feeling his cotton sweater's sleeve on the back of my neck while feeling his chest rise and fall with each breath. I wanted to be her, and I didn't entirely know why. At the thought of being in Jeremiah's embrace, I found myself trying to smell his cologne from across the table, watching as his smile sparkled from the overhead light illuminating his face each time he turned to talk to Daphne. I wanted to feel the heat of his body against mine, I wanted to know what it felt like to have his fingers inlaced with mine, making an unbreakable bond and being connected like they were.

Then it hit me, causing my mindless gaze on my plate to move to the unoccupied space on the back wall. "Oh my God; the guys in the magazine." I remembered seeing at Jeremiah's, "I was what that title said, I was what the bold letters said - GAY!"

My heart was breaking right in the middle of all of my friends, in the award's ceremony, as my mind replayed, "I'm Gay, I'm actually Gay!" I felt tears starting to brew in my eyes as I took a deep breath, trying to relieve some of my emotions without anyone noticing. Realizing the feelings I'd had over the past few months were an attraction. Not only an attraction but falling for my best friend; I couldn't wrap my mind on how the hell I could be a good Christian while secretly loving Jeremiah - a guy. My broken heart switched to immediate fear, thinking of hell's gates opening up and taking me down just at the idea of me being like the guys on that back cover. To keep myself from crying and releasing the heartbreak to my face, I stare up at Jeremiah and Daphne, her head now on his shoulder. Red-faced, feeling a hurt like never before, I look over their heads to the back wall behind the picked over buffet, counting down the minutes for all of this all to be over, trying to keep it all together.

"Donovan Shelton!" Upon hearing my name over the loudspeaker, I snap out of my daze, still somewhat misty eyed, and look at Coach Thomas, the source of my shock, confusion fixed on my face. "Come on up son, You deserve this." He says while leaning into the microphone that was attached to the podium, trying to get my attention. In my emotional rollercoaster, I had no idea why he was calling me up on stage, but I stood while everyone applauded, walking quickly to meet Coach Thomas in front of everyone. Reaching out my hand, I shake hands with Coach and turn to smile for a picture. My mother was now propped in the aisle in front of the podium on one knee, looking through the viewfinder of her Nikon camera. Snapping a barrage of pictures, trying to capture the perfect shot of this proud moment for years to come. Each flash from the camera leaves a blue square floater lingering in my sight. Looking down at the gold plated trophy, a silver engraved plate on the walnut wood base read, "Most Valuable Player." Now even more confused, I look at Coach Thomas, giving him a look of disbelief.

Turning to walk off the stage, Coach stops me with his broad hand on my shoulder. "Wait there a minute Van," Coach says while leaning into the microphone. "Everyone knows that playing a team sport can be difficult, but playing a team sport that you've never played a day of life, is even harder." He settles back on his heels, lowering his voice to a tolerable level. "Van rose to the challenge and overcame his lack of experience to be one of the Most Valuable Team members we have." He kept on while my cheeks began to warm, turning red in embarrassment. "Our team voted to select their MVP, and your team made sure to vote for someone who truly deserved it." Coach said while jutting a smile towards me. "Son, You worked really hard and we couldn't have done it without you." Lifting his hands to start the entire gymnasium into thunderous applause.

Returning to my seat, I stare at the trophy in full exasperation, not fully sure that this was real. I didn't even want to play soccer but to be told that I was actually good at it was a really rewarding moment. My chest began to fill with pride, my face plastered with a sheepish smile, pushing the tears away. As I look up and see Jeremiah and Daphne again, entangled in a loving embrace, smiling at me. My happiness escaped as quickly as it came, giving way to the hurt that had momentarily lapsed from my thoughts.

Before leaving the ceremony, where I won three trophies and received a framed certificate, I ran into the bathroom and stood in silence at the row of sinks as the door slowly closed behind me. Glaring at my reflection in the mirror, a tear fell down my face, landing on my cold hand that had turned white from clutching the corner of the light blue Formica countertop. Even with all of these awards, the applause and praise, the high-fives, and congratulations - the only thing I wanted, the only thing my heart desired, was smiling and laughing with his arms wrapped around someone else. No matter what I was, I would never be in Jeremiah's arms like she was and I had to accept that. No matter how hard it would be, I had to come to terms with the fact that I would never be loved like that by my best friend.

Chapter Thirteen

The pain of loving someone from afar can be crippling to your mind, body, and soul. Love doesn't have an alarm clock, or even a snooze button; you can't set it to go off when you want nor place it on a brief pause while life catches up. Watching someone you love freely and easily give another person the attention you so desperately yearn for, can drive a person mad. Every moment since coming to terms with my attraction to Jeremiah, I felt powerlessness to both my urges and pain. The one-sided intimacy replayed over and over again in my mind, causing my heart to break more each time. I regretted falling head-over-heels for this unobtainable guy, yet, knowing his own curiosity had been what unraveled the map to my discovery.

I longed to feel the electric pulses of another person's desires being in my control, while having that love returned to me and appreciated. Funny how just six months ago, I was just Donovan - a nerdy, band geek that loved to spend his time drawing and reading sci-fi books; and then now. To being the lonely, yearning, unknown gay guy of the group, unable to control his heart from getting more shattered each day. I didn't ask for these feelings or the person I was becoming. I wanted these feelings to stop, so I could be, what I thought, was normal again.

Turning down a red dirt road, deep in the countryside, on the north part of town, Bobbing and weaving the minivan, my mother rocks the vehicle side to side, trying to steer clear of the massive potholes and preventing damage to the front-end alignment. The road was carved into thick overgrown hay fields, situated at the base of the Brevard Mountain Range. On the edge of a thick grove of leafless oak trees, older mill houses begin to appear as my mother slows the minivan looking for my drop off. "2465..." My mother says, while reaching up to turn the radio down, studying each house number, trying to find Thomas' house.

"Here we go!" She says, turning into a small, single story white house with a covered wrap-around porch. Looking past the modest country farmhouse, Coach Thomas was in the garage, bent over a sun bleached, red faded four-wheeler. Seeing that we had arrived, Coach Thomas gave a friendly wave in our direction, as my mother looked for a place to park. "Hey Millie! Don't worry! The boys won't be on this thing." Coach Thomas jokes, walking from the garage to meet us in the side yard. "That thing has been busted since spring." I let out an audible, "Hallelujah" feeling reassured that I wouldn't end up with a broken bone or dead from my inability to handle an engine between my legs.

I didn't mind getting dirty like most southern boys, but we grew up poor. We didn't have mountain bikes or outdoor toys; I had a hand-me-down Huffy bicycle that belonged to my cousin, who graduated high school six years ago - not entirely sure on how old it was when he gave it to me when I was eight. I've never been on a four-wheeler, and I didn't want another weekend of first-time experiences to happen under the watchful gaze of "The Guys."

"Now listen, before you get out of this van," My mother says while unbuckling her seatbelt, "Same thing I said when you went to Davis', If I hear anything.." Cutting her off mid sentence, slinging my backpack over my shoulder, reaching for my sleeping bag from the back seat, "I know mom, you can trust me. You won't hear anything about me being disrespectful, I promise." I could tell my mother was about to rip into me for cutting her off but thankfully Ms. Patty walked out the side door of the house, waving for my mother to come in.

"Hey Millie! Before you leave, come in and have a cup of coffee or something." Politely declining, my mother was more of a sweet tea kind-a-girl, "Maybe next time Patty, I have to go get Emmalee from my sister-in-laws and get home before it gets too late. The awards ceremony ran over so she's probably already asleep, but thank ya though honey." With a final glare at me, followed by a loving smile, she puts the minivan in reverse and backs out the driveway. Rolling the driver's side window down as she situates herself on the road, she reaches out the window and gives a wave as she pushes the accelerator. Leaving the Thomas' in a trail of dust and taillights, leaving me alone in the driveway to carry all of my belongings up the stairs and into the house.

"The other fellas are in Colby's room. Down the hall, last room on the left. You boys can sleep in the living room. After me and Dave go to bed, we can't hear anything from the back of the house; so you boys have fun up front. But don't stay up too late, we have church in the morning." Ms. Patty says as I drop my sleeping bag on the sofa and head towards a crowd of voices in the back of the house.

Reaching the door to Colby's room, I hear Jeremiah's voice above the others. He was explaining how he and Daphne had decided to start dating, putting a halt to my steps. Knowing it was too late to turn and run home, I lay my head on the door, trying to calm my nerves before turning

Repentance of the Southern Burden | 85

the door knob and entering a room filled with chaos. While composing myself, the door abruptly swung open, causing me to lose my footing, making me stumble into the center of Colby's crowded bedroom. In my plummet, I narrowly missed his dresser that housed an old tube television, only to lock gazes with Jeremiah and Brody, who were sitting on the bed against the wall. Colby was now standing over me, apologizing for opening the door, making me tumble into the room, but my eyes never left Jeremiah's. Breaking my mortified embarrassments, we all have a good laugh at my expense. Settling down, we pulled out the various snacks and sodas we packed and started getting ready for a movie night in the living room.

"You guys cool with watching 'Gone in Sixty Seconds, or do you just want to watch tv?" Asked Colby as he fumbled through a stack of DVDs located on top of the entertainment center. "Ah man, I've been wanting to see that," says Brody, rolling his green camouflage sleeping back against the wall. "I'm game for whatever," Jeremiah follows, I just nod my head in agreement with the group, still unable to find my voice. Putting the DVD in and pressing play, Colby rolls his red sleeping bag out while Jeremiah follows on the opposite wall as Brody, only leaving one spot for me; between Colby and Jeremiah. Not wanting to complain about being claustrophobic, I roll my sleeping bag out and prop my pillow up against the sofa.

Forty-five minutes into the movie, everyone seemed to be bored with the Nicholas Cage drama, and started talking about the one thing most guys do when more than two of them are together - girls. "So, you are telling me..." Colby interrogates Jeremiah, "that you and Daphne are an item?" trying to get the full story straight from the horse's mouth. Full of arrogance, Jeremiah explains how he and Daphne were chatting on AOL Instant Messenger when she was out of town this summer. They started getting really close and before she came home, they were official.

I couldn't stop my stomach from churning at the word; official. The conversation seemed to go on forever between Colby and Jeremiah. Brody, who was uninterested in the drama, started dozing off. Unable to get comfortable, he asked if it was ok to give up the sleeping bag for Colby's bed. That left me, Jeremiah and Colby in the living room to continue the Lifetime movie drama that is Jeremiah and Daphne's apparent love affair. Having one less person in the small space did allow each of us to have a little bit more room, though none of us made the initiative to reposition our bags.

"So, have you gotten anymore….you know…from the garage?" Changing the subject, Jeremiah asks with a low-toned whisper, tilting his head towards the outside. I wanted to stop hearing about him and Daphne, but this wasn't a fair trade off. "Of course I have!" Colby sits up while remembering Brody, rolling his eyes, he slumps back down in his bag. "Brody is in my room, and he'll tell everyone." Jeremiah huffs, punching both fists to the floor. His disappointment paints a grimace across his face as the room falls silent.

Brody was younger than us by a year, but he was known for blabbing any given secret like most tweens do. "Tell me where it is!" Jeremiah snaps up from his bag, "I bet I can sneak in the room without him waking up." Already unzipping his sleeping bag and standing, confident in his spy skills. Getting the exact coordinates, Jeremiah stealthily tiptoes to Colby's room. Three minutes later, Jeremiah rounds the corner with a magazine tucked under his shirt. "Told ya!" He says while tossing the magazine on Colby's sleeping bag, high-fiving Colby as he slides back into his own bag. "We have to be quiet, Braydon is in his room and my parents are down the hall. If we hear anyone coming, we have three seconds too sling this in one of our bags, deal?" Colby looks at us both for our understanding of the rules and the clear "You got it" answers.

Reluctantly, I agreed. The last thing I wanted to see was one of those magazines, especially with what I knew was in the back cover. "Man, look at her boobs, they're bigger than my head!" Jeremiah exclaims, while pointing at the peroxide blonde on the cover. She was pushing her arms together, making her breast perkier with large, peach colored nipples, exposing her small waist, leaving nothing to the imagination. Flipping through the pages, Colby and Jeremiah seemed to be having the time of their lives, looking at all the positions and different types of women. Some were partially dressed in skirts, some in see-through lingerie, but most, completely naked. To my surprise, this magazine didn't seem to have a lot of guys in it, so maybe, just maybe, there wasn't the GAY section like the other one had. Without the temptation of seeing an exposed man's body, I wouldn't have to worry about getting a boner in front of them. Thankfully, none of this was doing anything for me, not even a slightest twitch below the belt. My arousal being pacified allowed me to relax a little as my friends enjoyed themselves.

Flipping to the last two pages, there it was - GAY. "DAMNNIT!" I thought to myself. I knew it was too good to be true. Trying not to look excited or perturbed, I look over Colby's shoulder, picking a spot on the wall to focus on, taking my focus from their laughing and the model's glossy muscles. "Man, I'm bigger than that guy," Says Colby, "and trust me, I look better too!"

***

*Pointing to a skinny, red haired young man on top of a muscular, tattooed bald guy, looking around my dad's age. Catching a peak of the page, causes my dick to electrify, realizing quickly that my worry was unwarranted. We were each in our own sleeping bags so no one could see that I was almost fully hard and touching myself.

Closing the magazine, sliding it down into his bag for safe keeping, Colby props himself up against the sofa with an idea, "Let's play truth or dare!" He says while looking at me for signals of a yes or a no. Before I could say anything, Jeremiah blurts out, "Hell yea! But serious ones. I don't want no kindergarten type of dares, we're almost sixteen and we can handle it." We all agree to his requirement and start contemplating what the first truth or dare should be, and to whom.

"Ok, I'll start." Colby leans over, looking straight at me. "Van, truth or dare," Colby asked, with hope in his voice that I would pick dare. Unfortunately for him, I say "truth". Both of the guys groan and huff while trying to come up with a truth for me to answer. Colby snaps his finger, causing me and Jeremiah to jump, "Ok! I got it. So, if you had to make out with anyone in the teen group, who would it be?" I sit back against my pillow, trying to think of any girl in our group that would work as a cop out that would satisfy their testosterone induced probing. I exclaimed, "Ashley Cooper!" Sadly for her, the probability of that would never happen. Both of their eyes widened and started loudly gawking in unison. "Dude, she would let you too!. Now you pick one of us." Colby says, pointing at him and Jeremiah.

Not sure if I wanted to know where this game was going to lead, I asked Jeremiah, truth or dare. He picks dare, and Colby bursts into daring him to walk in the kitchen and get a gatorade out of the fridge, butt-naked. Letting out a nervous laugh, I secretly adjusted my package knowing this could set me over the edge. "I'm not scared!" He snobbishly says, while getting out of his sleeping bag, dropping his shorts and running to the kitchen. Yanking the refrigerator door open, he grabs the gatorade, and runs back jumping back into his sleeping bag. I noticed he didn't put

Repentance of the Southern Burden | 89

his shorts back on when he reached his bag. He was now laying in his bag naked, with no plans of dressing. The thought of his naked body rubbing the warm fleece of the bag made my rod start leaking through my shorts. I knew I would be picked next, so I tried to check to see if I had a wet spot on my shorts from my cock's excitement, but in the dark, I couldn't tell.

"Colby, truth or dare?" Asked Jeremiah. Relieved that I dodged the question this time, but the relief quickly turned to panic as Colby answered dare. "I dare you to climb into Van's sleeping back and act like you're having sex." Jeremiah says while sitting up higher out the top of his sleeping bag with an "I bet you won't do it" tone to his voice. Looking over at me, Colby gets out of his sleeping bag and motions for me to open mine to allow him entry. Aware of my current situation, I knew he would feel my hardness, but reluctantly, I allowed him in my bag and turned my back to him. Making him spoon me as he dry humps my backside. We all laugh, as Colby mimics rapid sexual maneuvers, fully clothed in my sleeping bag for thirty seconds. As he's sliding out of my bag, Colby reaches around, grazing his hand over the front of my shorts. My breath caught in my chest, not sure of what to say, and with that small touch, my head started spinning.

This was the first time someone had touched my manhood besides me, even though it was probably by accident, it still sent a shock through my spine. Colby didn't seem to notice as he sat on the couch, looking down at Jeremiah and myself, still in our bags. "Truth or dare." Again, I repeat, "Truth." Obviously, not the answer they wanted because they both began to protest and tease. "NO! NO! NO! Now come on, we've both done a dare, you can do a dare." Challenges Colby, pointing at him and Jeremiah. "Fine!" Giving into peer pressure, "you win, dare" terrified at how fast all this was going, feeling it was getting out of control.

"I dare you to do the same thing I did to you, but with Jeremiah and do it NAKED - Both of you!" he says while falling back on the sofa with a playful low laugh. Looking at Jeremiah with panic on my face, he shrugs his shoulders, and says, "I'm game, are you?" Colby and Jeremiah were both staring at me as I carefully positioned my raging boner into the waistband of my shorts. A failed attempt to hide how engorged I was from all this attention. I sheepishly walk over to Jeremiah's sleeping bag and climb in. Before I get into position, Colby protests that we weren't naked, just as Jeremiah twirls his blue shorts over his head, throwing them on the couch. Leaving me being the only one clothed in the cotton-lined bag, inches from his naked body. Reluctantly, I slide my shorts down to my ankles and over my feet. Reaching down, I pull them out and throw them in the same direction as Jeremiah had thrown his. Assuming the dared position, Jeremiah got behind me, wrapping his arms around my waist, pulling me into his warm body.

Yearning to be in his arms at the awards ceremony was nothing compared to what I was experiencing. His toned arms grazing my hip bones, his nipples, erect from the cool exposed air, tickled my shoulder blades. His breath, warm and nervous on my neck caused pure and total submission to him. My swollen dick, completely unobstructed, threatening to explode at the mere touch of another person.

Finding the ideal dominating position, he starts the motions that Colby had done but was slow and steady, savoring each pass his body made to my submissive flesh. I could fill his veiny member sliding between my thighs, getting thicker and bigger as the head of his cock gently tapped the underside of my balls. The sensation sent intoxicating shocks through my body, making my eyes roll into the back of my head. My body tensed, which tightened my thighs around his now fully hard dick, making Jeremiah let out a long, enjoyable, release of air.

Though he wasn't actually in me, it felt like we were actually experiencing a form of sex for the first time, simply by the friction made with my thighs. Each thrust caused my thighs to tighten, leaving a wet trail from his leaking cock each time he reared back. His speed quickened with each lunge, until his breath and attention became more powerful and determined. Noticing the obvious pleasure on Jeremiah's face, Colby curiously asked, "Does that feel like actual sex?" I was taken back by his question. Knowing all three of us were virgins, how would we know? Jeremiah abruptly stops and answers with a staggered breath, "Dude, it feels really good. Donovan, how about for you?" he asked while leaning into me, making his slim toned body lay completely flat against my back. With a teetering, breathy voice, I say, "Ah yeah, actually it does feel really good." Colby stands, a noticeable tented cock protruding out, leaving a wet spot on his plaid shorts. "Ok! I have to see this for myself!" demanding that he get a chance to know the ecstasy that my body was providing. Climbing into the sleeping bag with Jeremiah and myself, Colby pulls his shorts off and throws them on the sofa and instructs me to turn over, giving his full access to my backside again but this time; no fabric as a barrier.

Now face to face with my heart's desire, my boner flashes up, poking Jeremiah in his stomach as Colby positions behind me. Shifting his hips, he aligns his body to cradle my ass. Using my now pre-cum lubricated thighs, he slowly pushes his fully engorged cock between my thighs. The slipping and tightness provided by my thighs causes Colby to release a long, involuntary, "Ahhhh" from deep inside his diaphragm. Understanding now why Jeremiah was pounding my body like a madman.

Enjoying the sensation, Colby loses all reluctance, wrapping both arms around my waist, pulling me close to his chest, not allowing an inch of my backside to be exposed to open air. In his embrace, I noticed how his body felt quite different to Jeremiah's. Colby was more muscular, though slightly shorter than me, but had a cock similar to Jeremiah's, but a lot thicker. I was in euphoria - not knowing what to do other than to turn occasionally with their request, giving them both ample time to use me. In the midst of the testosterone clouded room, they asked if I wanted to try feeling the motions with one of them. I declined each offer to change roles, because I was enjoying being the "monkey in the middle" and submitting to their desires. My pleasure was already coursing through my veins by simply being used for their needs.

Turning to face Colby to give Jeremiah another round of my thighs, Jeremiah slams between my thighs, erratically thrusting, going faster and faster. Each pounding motion, sliding my body in the bag, closer and closer to Colby's sweaty body, until our bodies were pressed to the zipper of the bag. My dick pressed up against Colby's stomach, leaving a large wet spot at his navel. Noticing the slippery wetness between us, I looked down, concerned that Colby would protest. Only to look up and find Colby's eyes, dilated and locked on my face.

Ignoring the mimicked motions behind me, Colby focuses his full attention on me. His hazel eyes refused to look away, almost giving me a come-hither look. Feeling the sliding on his stomach, as Jeremiah continues his thrusting between my thighs, Colby closes his eyes, and leans in for a full, open mouthed, unexpected kiss. His tongue darts into my mouth, loping my tongue around his as his inhibitions release a longing moan. Wrapping his left hand around my neck, he pulls me in tighter, accepting him through my lips and into my trembling mouth as our messy kissing gets more and more intense.

Jeremiah, seeing this surprised display of affection, picks up his pace. His intense vigor caused his dick to thicken and get wetter. Colby's passionate kissing kept my body tense, giving Jeremiah even more grip around his cock. Jeremiah holds his breath as his final hard smack into my body gives the last electric pulse he needed. Jeremiah starts spewing rope after rope of a warm, thick liquid; coating the underside of my taint. The warmth and wetness sends me over the edge and with my cock still pinned against Colby's stomach, I explode the largest load of my life. Still smashed due to the lack of space in my sleeping bag, Colby never released his grip on my neck or his attention to my lips. The first rope of cum travels from the head of my cock and hits Colby on the chin, followed by five more spurts of cum, between the narrow space of our sweaty bodies.

Looking down, at our soaked stomachs, Colby pulls me in with more determination, as his lips part more, head tilted back, and eyes closed, reveling in this shared experience. Balls tightened, Colby begins firing shot after shot of thick cum on my already dripping stomach. One after another, until every inch of my front was soaked. The three of us went limp from exhaustion, and pleasure. Covered in sweat and semen, the post orgasm high circled the room, unable to release its grip on the three of us. Our breath slowly returns to normal, our muscles relax, separating our entanglement, as we all roll to our backs and stare at the ceiling, unable to move or put into words what our bodies had just experienced.

Before sliding out of my sleeping bag, Colby leans in, giving me another passionate kiss followed by a trail of sensual peaks. Unzipping the bag, he stands, revealing the full sight of his cock, inches from my face. Reaching around the couch, Colby grabs three paper towels and hands them to each of us to clean up. "Well, that was unexpected but oh my God, definitely fun. We will have to do that again," said Colby while bending to pick up his shorts from beside the recliner. Jeremiah says nothing, just like before. Not moving his gaze from the ceiling as he cleanses his body of any evidence of our truth-or-dare gone awry. I look up at Colby, still undressed, as he bends down, narrowing the gap to the floor where I was laying, to give me one last soft peck.

As we started to get dressed and discard the drenched paper towels, my mind took off. How was this different from the first time with Jeremiah? Why did I feel fulfilled by simply being passed around between the two of them? It wasn't really sex, but more like friction and libido. Then, it hit me; this had been majorly different. Colby wanted me to enjoy it as much as he did. Not only that, but he kissed me; not once, or twice, but he opened his mouth, directed me to open mine, and explored my body. He gifted me an abundance of passionate kisses, like those I had only seen in movies. He was worried about me, and worried about my experience being just as important as his. My head couldn't wrap around how he was so different from Jeremiah; different and better.

Now that everyone was cleaned off and dressed, We settled in our bags, picked our snack of choice out of the pile, and turned the TV on. Reruns of TV Land played over the steamy living room as I sat alone in my wet sleeping bag, staring dazed at the ceiling. "Come share my sleeping bag with me, if you want since yours is all messy now," whispers Colby, unzipping his bag, flipping it open, showing that he had his shorts on and had plenty of room for both of us. Without hesitation, I leave the wet confines of my own bag, giving my body a final wipe down with a paper towel and sliding in front of Colby. Zipping it closed and I pull my pillow over from my bag and slide it under my head.

Nuzzling my pillow, trying to calm my nerves, I feel a muscular arm slowly reach around my waist under the concealment of the sleeping bag. Pulling me in close, Colby situates my body to cradle against his bare chest. My heart thudded as my body became intertwined with his. I was now feeling the same confused emotion from Jeremiah but now with another friend. But this time - completely different, I melted. I allowed my body to be engulfed by his. I took in his scent, wanting my brain to never forget this feeling. The feeling of being wanted and in the arms of

Repentance of the Southern Burden | 95

someone who wanted me.

Colby was passionate, thoughtful, loving and was treating me special. I was like Daphne - swooning in the arms of a strong man. Finding sleep approaching quickly I snuggled down into the shared sleeping bag, Colby's cock deflating behind me.**

***

Looking through my heavy eyelids across the room, I see my first love, Jeremiah, laughing at something Lucy did to Ricky on the TV. "This could have been you," I thought. But honestly, not caring enough to tell him, because for the first time - someone was caring for me. Someone reached for me, provided my pleasure and ensured I was ok. In that moment, I felt loved.

Flashing in my mind, my eyes slammed open, and worry sat in. "If only in the morning, I wasn't discarded like before with Jeremiah," I thought. Was this just guy stuff or did Colby want more? Or was he just using me like Jeremiah had? Too tired to allow room for any more thoughts, I just relaxed down, knowing only the morning sunlight would tell. I didn't want to spoil this moment with worry. I wanted the feeling of being in a man's arms, and I wanted it to be branded in my memory forever.

Slowing my breath, peaceful sleep begins approaching. On my last thought before releasing this moment as a memory, I think, "This couldn't have been a dream, because my dreams could never be this good." As all the tension leaves my body, sleep wins over my mind, as I slip into a dream world, while nestled in the muscular arms of Colby Thomas.

Chapter Fourteen

Discovery can happen not just by sight and sensation, but your actions - your experiences. Discovery can be a relief at times, just knowing that what you have worked for and tried to find; has been found and validated. In the frantic search, lessons are learned, showing you that what you have been searching for, was there all along. Sometimes simply placed in the most obscured, unexpected places. In many cases, found not by your own hands, but through the actions of someone else's. A bystander who is oblivious to the struggles you've endured, however, easily solved by their mere presence. But, discovery can come at a price.

Christmas was rapidly approaching in two weeks, and I, like every Sunday before, found myself walking into the Pepto Bismol colored halls of Heritage Baptist. Now flanked in gold and greenery with wreaths everywhere and an eighteen foot perfectly decorated Christmas Tree in the vestibule. Heritage Baptist was making sure that if you weren't in the Christmas spirit, this place would remind you of the importance at every corner. Making my way into the men's restroom, I stop at the sight of four large wreaths above each urinal and toilet.

"Really?" I thought, "this is where they want you to think about the

Savior's birth? While relieving yourself of the stale, reheated and burnt Sunday school coffee?" Knowing this would be my last chance to use the restroom before the start of church, I knew I better make sure that I did my business now or risk being uncomfortable.

While in the restroom, my mind began to wonder, using the silence of the cold room to allow my thoughts to bounce around in my head. Thinking back to the night at Colby's, and the emotions that had now attached themselves to the memories. We went our separate ways at church that next morning, sitting with our families. Teen Church was canceled so that everyone could be together for the final sermon of Pastor Rich's series called "Pushing Away From Sin." The final of a five part series, each connecting to the previous week's lesson. Each Individual sermon is meant to help the masses gain the strength to push away from the worldly sins that surround us. Bringing us closer to our faith while gaining tools to defend against the world.

"God has placed these obstacles in your path to test you - to bring you closer to his forgiving arms." Pastor Rich says, leaning into the pulpit, projecting his voice, which echoed off the back walls and high vaulted ceilings of the grand sanctuary. "These obstacles are things that you may think are harmless, but NO!" Slamming his fist to the oak carved pulpit with a loud bang, causing me to unintentionally let out a short laugh under my breath at everyone jumping at the percussion. My lapse in judgment of the timing, prompting a scornful gaze from my mother at the end of my pew. A gaze that told me, "Stop immediately" or she would "reach" for a hymnal in pew back in front of me, only to leave a bruise on my arm from one of her epically painful church pinches as punishment.

Collecting myself, I clear my throat and lift my head as Pastor Rich starts putting all the pieces of what he was teaching into moving forward as a church and how to grow closer in our faith. "Today, we as followers of God are at the greatest risk! We know from his word that these risks are sins. Society wants all of us to turn a blind eye to what the scriptures tell us are wrong, sinful behaviors. Your neighbors want you to believe that using the Lord's name in vain is ok. Your co-worker wants you to engage in conversations that lead you down a path of disgust and impurity." Looking at my watch, I notice the time getting closer to 12:00pm. Pastor Rich would have to wrap it up by then or people would get restless at the thought of the ever-growing long lines at their choice of restaurant for the after-church crowd.

My attention was slapped back to Pastor Rich with his last point on social perils, "And the television - the most harmful avenue for perversions. Hollywood wants us to believe and laugh with a storyline that shows your family…." he pauses, raising his voice with more determination, "Our kids! That homosexuality is ok! They can make money on the back of the non-believer, but not in my house! No siree!" He says, while shaking his head side to side. "We will not celebrate the lifestyle of two women or two men, engaging in what our scriptures tell us is a sin!"

Pastor Rich leans back onto his heels while releasing his grip on the pulpit, the confirmation of the congregation's understanding was heard all around me with a rousing "Amen" bouncing from every corner of the room. I sat frozen - feeling his words stabbing me, burning with each probe. The voids filled with fear and doubt.

Even though he wasn't looking directly at me, he seemed to know exactly what I had done and he was making damned sure that I knew God wasn't happy. I couldn't help looking near the front to where Colby was sitting with his family and then on the opposite side of the sanctuary to Jeremiah's. Both guys were stirring in their seats, from the same guilt billowing in their guts as mine. At the end of that service, we didn't meet up and chat, we didn't even acknowledge each other existed; we just went with our families to continue our lives as if nothing happened. Unable to shake what was shoved down my throat by Pastor Rich, I excuse myself from my parent's to go and wait in the minivan to go home. Each passing second, the guilt kept growing and growing. On the verge of a breakdown, I see my mother and father approaching. Quickly, I put away my worries and gather myself. On the ride home, I fake a happy exterior while trying to maintain the conversation. Unknown to my parents, my internal struggles were getting overwhelming and unable to cage.

More Sundays passed with no conversations or connections between Colby, Jeremiah and myself. Honestly, I felt it was all because of our religious guilt from doing something the scriptures taught was wrong. I couldn't understand how something could connect me closer to them but could push me farther from my beliefs. I felt like I was walking away, each day, another step away from God and my faith. "The Guys" went on with our lives as normal as we could, without any validating of what we had done and accepted where it left us.

Washing my hands to leave the bathroom before the Annual Christmas Cantata, knowing it would be the last time I had the chance of a break. I open the door, almost knocking yet another Christmas wreath to the floor as the door shuts behind me. Rounding the corner to take the long way down the hallway to reach my seat with my sister, I bump into Colby. Causing him to drop his leather bible and gatorade on the ground. While apologizing, both of our hands reach for the half-full red sports drink Colby had dropped. Our hands briefly touch, sending a wave of memories and a longing feeling that I'd missed since that night.

"Aw man! I'm so sorry, I didn't…" cutting me off, Colby stands and places his free hand up between us to stop me. "Man, you're good, there's no way you could have seen me. Are you ok?" He asks as I step back, giving him more room. "Um, yeah, I'm fine! You good?" taking this moment to just bask in the fact that this was the closet I had been to him in a month. "Yeah, I'm good." He continues, "I, ahh, well… It's been crazy lately, and we've missed you at the Teen Services. What made you decide to stay in the main services on Sunday mornings?" He asked, while stepping forward to fill the space I had given him. "Mom and Dad are both now in the choir, and they wanted me to sit and keep an eye on Emmalee. Apparently, she was getting into trouble in her Sunday school class, so I am now her appointed prison guard." Partially lying, but with some truthfulness in my voice, I allow my words to trail from my lips in hopes of ending the awkwardness of our compromised position.

"I understand that, but maybe after Christmas you can come back to the Youth Service." Colby says, looking up with a half-tilted smile, "I know, you are missed. I mean, I … ah.." His words stutter with a vulnerable voice. "Ah..I miss you." My heart leapt into my throat. Unable to look me in the eyes, he says, "I miss hanging out with you…in the services, you know," staring at his feet, his cheeks beginning to turn pink. "Trust me, It's so boring in the main service and I miss the upbeat music and group activities with the teens. Everyone in here just sits and stands and then that's it; everyone shakes hands and leaves." I say, trying to move the conversation along, noticing the color remaining in his cheeks. We talked for a brief moment, in our own world, oblivious to the timeline of events for the day as the organ and piano start playing, waking us both up from our chance collision of fate.

"Ah crap! We're going to be late!" I belt out to Colby in panic. "This is going to be so boring! I'm going to warn you, my parent's look horrible in those makeshift Bible character costumes. Try not to laugh!" Jokingly, I say, trying to walk past him in a rush to find my seat before the lights go down. With a smile, I turn to look back at him as he laughs at my obvious joke on my parent's behalf. Turning back around to continue down the hall, Colby calls out to me, causing me to stop, mid step.

"Hey Van! Catch you after the cantata?" Apparently, waiting for a response before finding his own seat, I quickly replied, "Yeah! Find me out front when it's over. We can chat then." Leaving him left a void in my chest. I wanted to be next to him, in his presence, but for now I resolved to just make my way through the double doors of the main sanctuary. The large room was bustling with people trying to find the best seat in the house to get a full view of the stage and choir. Seeing my family, halfway up the center, I wave to my cousins, as I walk by, trying to force the lump in my chest to recede before I have to endure three hours of music and Baptist theater. I was scared to let the feelings of Colby leave my heart. I didn't want to release the feeling of being wanted, or maybe even at some point, having the possibility of feeling someone's love directed at me. But for now, I had to file them away to a hidden corner of my mind. I knew my attention was needed for the production and having the visions of that night now would prove to be more of a problem than a pleasure. I didn't want to spoil my memories; I wanted to preserve them.

Chapter Fifteen

Finding my seat, next to my cousins and my sister, I sat, trying to make myself as comfortable as possible with the now added room in our pew. There were no adults sitting with us, seeing as though all our parents were in the cantata that depicted the birth of Jesus. Three hours of blasting music, mediocre solos, and choir over singing; this would definitely be a pain for both my eyes and my ears. As the lights dim down for the start of the cantata, my mind wanders at what Colby wanted to talk to me about? He hadn't made any attempt to talk to me since that morning after being in his arms all night, but now he wants to talk? The confusion was swirling around my head as the bright lights flashed in a spotlight on the choir and stage.

Even with the main lights off in the sanctuary, the spot light was bright enough to allow my eyes to dart around the sanctuary, searching for any type of stimuli. Easily, I found Colby and his dad sitting to my left near the front with their family all around them. A lot of new faces, assuming friends and family of Ms. Patty's, who had a solo at the beginning of the play. Anyone that had a chance to hear her sing, wouldn't want to miss her renowned soprano tones belting out over the sanctuary, filling the room with her angelic operatic vibrato. Even in the dim light, the shadows of his muscularity and broad shoulders were the mirror images of his father's. But in contrast to his father, Colby's muscles were encased in a tight red knit sweater and green button up collar.

Feeling a smile reach my face - the music blared, obviously louder than it should. As the sound man turned the music to a tolerable level, we all settled in for a moving dramatization of what we Christians believe were the days leading to the birth of Jesus Christ. I knew this story front and back - uninterested I allowed my eyes to wander the room, people watching in my attempts to stay awake.

The lights dim down to the room echoing with "Hallelujah's" and "Amens" from the audience, feeling, what we call, "The Holy Spirit." I call it, "Everyone look at me." Yelling out-loud in church, regardless of what you were saying, always made me more irritated, not more Christian. The sound guy switches music tracks to a harp playing soft music as a single spot light illuminates a spot on the stage. It was Jeremiah! He was standing alone dressed in a brown and cream wiseman costume, looking like he had on a one piece dress made of bedsheets and rags. His blue eyes sparkled with the spot light as he clutched to the gold and jewel encrusted box in his hands.

"They traveled to Nazareth by way of Bethlehem. Mary and Joseph tired with their travels and Mary's due date approaching." He projected, "Finding nowhere to rest, they found a stable of hay, knowing that soon her baby, our savior, would be here. Surrounded by sheep and cattle, a star brightly shone in the sky, guiding the wisemen to their side. Shepards rejoiced as the world realized that our savior was born." Jeremiah says, very well rehearsed, and looking very uncomfortable at being center stage. Finishing his lines, he turns and walks off of the stage to the side to join his mother and the other choir members as the play continues to depict the moment the wisemen arrived at Mary and Joseph's side.

Even though you could tell he was nervous, he did great. I couldn't help but smile in pride at his monologue and confidence. Jeremiah didn't sing with the choir but became an extra in all of the town scenes and motions behind the members that were the "actors" of the different parts of the play. Moving around the stage, in various parts, I felt a fuzzy feeling in my stomach. Releasing a feeling, long dormant over the past few weeks. I hadn't given much thought to Jeremiah since Colby had filled the void and provided pleasure to me when Jeremiah discarded my feelings. Why was I so damned attached to him even though I knew I would never get anything from him like I had Colby?

Watching his magnificent performance, I noticed his eyes sparkled each time he looked up to the crowd. He surveyed the crowd of church goers, shoulder to shoulder, all engrossed in the group's performance. His presence placed me in a trance like state, making me search for him each time the lights came back up. I spent the entire cantata following his every movement as if he was the lead actor and was responsible for telling the entire story by himself.

The cantata ended with a drawn out version of the Hallelujah Chorus and an exhausted cast and choir. As the last music note was still bouncing around the vaulted sanctuary, everyone stands and erupts into applause and amen's. Pastor Rich approached the center stage, and led everyone through his closing thoughts. He congratulated the group of church volunteers for their hard work and ended the cantata with a closing prayer.

The lights returned to their normal brightness, as everyone gathered their belongings and the performers walked off the stage to the main floor. Making sure to not lose my sister in the gaggle of people, who weren't eager to leave, I wait for my parent's to congratulate everyone on a job well done. Hoping they would be quick, so I could go and meet

Colby out front as I promised. As my mother approached us, my sister broke my grip on her hand, running to hug my mother in her cream colored floor length costume. Catching my mother in mid stride, she leans down, careful to not cause the fabric over her hair to fall to the floor.

"Oh babydoll, did you like it?" Ask my mother, searching for any type of validation from her children. I knew my mother hated the costume she was forced to wear, it was poorly made and was constructed of the most unflattering bolt of materials. I'm sure the fabric was in the clearance bin at the local bulk fabric store and was made as a cheap way to look the part for the cantata. "Yeah! It was great mom!" I say giving a truly sincere smile, leaning in to give her a big hug on top of my leg-latched sister. "You guys were amazing, Mom! I know you weren't trying to stand out, but I could pick out your voice above everyone else and you sounded great!" My mother's cheeks rush with a dark pink hue as she leans in and plants a small kiss on my forehead. "Honey, I'm glad you enjoyed it, it was definitely a lot of work but it was worth it." Shifting my sister from her legs, she continues, "Don't let me forget, I have a surprise for you," she says while smiling and lifting her brows. "I was talking with Ms. Patty in the choir room during rehearsal, and I agreed to something that I'm sure you'll be head-over-heels to do." Giving no more clues, she turns to a group of ladies behind her, anxiously awaiting to share their admiration for her and the rest of the choir's valiant efforts.

Looking at my mother, I see a woman who has no problems with busting through the doors of a group to join in a social circle, but also a woman who had the same insecurities plaguing her as I did. She didn't want to be center stage or have a solo. She only wanted to make sure she had a place on the outskirts of the group and have the feeling of belonging. Seeing her smile and watching her body language convey a sense of pride for her hard work made me see how much I looked up to her - and envied her. Even playing a small part, she put herself out there in the light and made herself be seen; and she was seen. By everyone in the sanctuary, but most importantly by me, her son. She didn't have to have a lead role to be important; she was just happy with being a part of something bigger than herself.

Chapter Sixteen

Belonging was one of my biggest fears at Heritage Baptist and in life. By being involved in this new church, with the possibility of actually making new friends, that fear continued to grow. Belonging is something that I never was lucky enough to feel in a church, or in life in general. In my family, I wasn't the rugged boy; I didn't like hunting, getting dirty or even being rowdy. I always was the weakest cousin when we wrestled on the trampoline, and always the last one picked on a team.

In high school, I was an outcast. The person that was rarely asked to sign a yearbook. I wasn't surrounded by jocks and cheerleaders dawning the school colors in any type of school team jersey. I was the guy with the least amount of pictures in the yearbook. I wasn't the guy who would score the winning touchdown at the homecoming game. I did have friends though; mostly friends like me. People who were just trying to blend into the walls of every class; trying to bide their time in high school until they could run from its doors, never to return again.

But in this church I was seen as a different person. This group of people, all gathered under the umbrella of a similar faith, gave me a place to belong and grow. Breaching the doors each Sunday made me feel like I was important and wanted. The church members, some old and some young, were all excited to see me walk in and join them. Yes, there were sports and the unquestionable cliques that naturally happen in a group, but everyone seemed to be welcoming. At church, I felt valid and necessary regardless of the personal turmoil of my day-to-day life. I easily forgot about blending in the walls of my high school because at the church, I was included, involved and wanted. This feeling was new to me but at the same time it fed my need to feel that I was in the right place and with the right people.

Remembering my promise to Colby, I asked my mother, who was completely surrounded by the Ladies Auxiliary Group, if I could meet her and my father out in front of the church after they got changed and were ready to head home. Giving me permission, I zigzagged through the hoards of people congregating at the front altar; half of the people were dressed normally while the other half in floor length costumes. Slowly making my way to the vestibule, I pushed open the heavy wooden door releasing a bitter cold breeze that slapped around my unjacketed body. The sudden drop in temperature sent chills all over my body. Looking around the front of the church searching for Colby, I see him at the flower bed standing to the side of the front door near the parking lot.

"Told ya I'd find ya!" I say, causing Colby to jolt at not seeing me approach. "Holy crap man! Again, I didn't see you! I swear, either I need glasses or you need to wear bells or something." Colby says, while holding his chest with a bent over laugh. "I'm sorry man, didn't mean to scare you." I say, laughing through my words at the sight of Colby seeming on edge. "Your mom did amazing! I knew she could sing, but holy crap, she belted it out today!"

Smiling at my compliment towards his mother, Colby rolls his eyes, and starts telling me how his mother had been practicing her solo for months. To the point that he and his father knew each word of the song, and how thankful he was that the cantata was over.

Changing the subject, Colby reveals what he wanted to talk about. "So mom and dad like to do a trip to Sugar Mountain after each Christmas to go skiing at my uncle's place. He and my aunt are always gone for work or at their beach house so each year he lets us use the place and have a quick vacay before school starts back" he continues, 'this year, my parents said I could bring some friends." A rush of blood soars from my feet through the top of my head, causing my body to let out an involuntary, full body shiver. Seeing what he thought was my body reacting to the cold air, Colby exclaims, "Dude! It's freezing out here! Where's your jacket?" Since I had forgotten my jacket inside the church on our family's pew, I was only wearing a button up long sleeved shirt.

Seeing my obvious discomfort, Colby stands and pulls his red sweater over his head, bending down to narrow the gap between us. He wraps the warmed oversized sweater around my shoulders, making sure every inch of my upper body is covered and shielded from the night air. The last lingering scent of his cologne enveloped around me, filling my nostrils with the sweet, musty scent of Abercrombie & Fitch Fierce cologne. Instinctively, I fold my arms to bring the provided warmth to my now numb limbs and wrap myself in his generosity.

He continues with his reasoning for this private chat, "So, I asked mom about having you and maybe Jeremiah come with us this time." My mouth froze open while my mind was trying to rationalize what he was asking me. I wondered if this is what my mother was hinting at. Sitting on the edge of the retaining wall of the flower bed he motions for me to follow his lead, sliding closer in efforts to steal some of his body heat and show my interest in his question. "It would be the week of New Years. They do an awesome fireworks show from the top of the mountain and we just ski and play cards all week. It's a lot of fun. Do you think you would want to come along?" I could see the excitement in his eyes, and hear his voice, longing for the next two weeks to pass so he could be there on the ski slopes.

"You wouldn't have to bring anything! I even have extra ski gear that you can use, so you won't have to rent any." Colby says, noticing my hesitation. He knew me well enough to know I was wondering what this trip would cost my parents or that I didn't have the necessary equipment. Registering that he was anxiously waiting for my response, I let out an excited, "Heck yeah!" Nodding my head in full confidence without the actual approval of my parents. "Heck Yeah! I would love that man! Thank you for thinking of me! I've never been skiing but I've always wanted to try. Just have to ask my parents and see if they are ok with it, and I can let you know."

Shifting himself to allow our thighs to touch, he sends an electric shock through my leg. Looking up from my daze, I can see he had planned ahead for my reply. "Oh, I asked mom to talk to you mom. I think she said yes, but yeah, check with them and I'll talk to Jeremiah and make sure we're all good," he says. "Usually we leave the day after Christmas and come back after the first. So, we will have a full week of "The Guys".

My body trembled at the excitement of thinking of "The Guys" again. I had put the thought of "The Guys" into the back of my mind, thinking that it had ended after that night in Colby's living room. Taking my trembling as a sign I was still cold, Colby leaned in wrapping his arm around my shoulders while giving me a tight hug and offering friction to my left forearm. Again, I start to melt at the chance of being nestled into the arms of this muscular guy who, for some reason, made sure I was always ok.

Repentance of the Southern Burden | 111

Before I could enjoy this bond for too long, Colby jokingly leans away saying, "Dude, you better get inside and find your coat - you better not get sick before we go!" Standing up to meet his parents who were now coming out the front doors of the church to head home, left me alone on the retaining wall. In my sadness of him leaving, I realize I still have his sweater. "Hey! Colby! Here's your sweater!" I say, starting to pull it off from around my shoulders. Still walking with his parents, he looks back over his shoulder, and yells back, "No worries, Just bring it with you when you come for the trip, that way you can stay warm if you don't find your jacket!" And with an accomplished smile on his face, he turned and continued his stride with his parents to their car until he vanished into the darkness of the parked cars.

Wrapping my arms tight around my body, I allow the last fragments of his scent to fill my soul. I realized, in that moment, that I was warm and cozy. Not from the thick woven threads of the red sweater, but by the feelings permeating from within my own body. For just one second, I didn't care about anything else in the world; I just wanted to keep taking all this in and allow the feeling to wash over me. The fresh essence of his smell surrounded my body and filled my head. With dreams of allowing him to entangle me in an embrace full of acceptance and belonging, and maybe even love. How could something this pure be wrong in the eyes of the Lord and the church? How could feeling these feelings be any different in a traditional relationship than what I was feeling now? It wasn't fair that God would deprive me from finally feeling like I mattered to someone, and that person wanted to make sure I was cared for.

I was falling hard yet again, but this time I had a memento. I had something of his to cherish, even if only for a few weeks, but it made the anticipation of the trip even more exhilarating. I hoped to experience more firsts on this trip, but I'd be happy with the same thing from that night in the living room. I knew I wanted more exploration and discovery with Colby, But Jeremiah would be there too. How would I deal with having my first real crush around me and still enjoy the person that hadn't pushed me away? Would Jeremiah object to me going? What if something did happen, would Colby ever open himself up and tell me that he felt something for me or would I just continue to be their "monkey-in-the-middle?" Only time would reveal, and I had a few weeks to finalize my plan before being alone with the only two people I had allowed to see my vulnerability. Even though I was impatient for more discovery, I knew they held the control to when, where and how the revelations would happen and I was for once, ok with releasing the control and following someone else's lead.

Chapter Seventeen

When you value something, your actions show that it's worthwhile and you protect it. Value can be placed on anything from diamonds, houses to cars and even people. A person should always have value. If not within themselves, then by the actions or words from others, who hold them in great esteem. Not only did I feel valued by Colby but I also felt wanted. I didn't feel like just an option or an experiment; I felt that he wanted my attention and my time and that was priceless to me.

Since being wrapped in Colby's sweater, I knew what I valued. I valued the slowly fading scent of his cologne, barely clinging to the fibers of his borrowed red sweater. I valued how big the sweater seemed on me, showing how strong Colby was in comparison to me. And I valued how when I snuggled his sweater to my face, I felt him close to me like he was in the sleeping bag that night. I found myself spending nights dreaming of Colby and I on the skiing trip when out of nowhere, he sweeps me up in his arms and confesses his love for me. Only to awaken, knowing I had binged watched too much Lifetime TV to allow my brain to fully make a clear and realistic plan for this upcoming ski trip.

Christmas morning had arrived with my sister running into my room, like every year before, yelling for me to get up and see all the presents under the tree. She was twelve years old, but her enthusiasm for Christmas made me think she was still writing letters to the North Pole. "Come on dumb butt! Get up!" Emmalee yells, while pulling my foot, left out from under my comforter, used for temperature control. Her icy hands made my leg retract, pulling my foot under the mound of blankets and sheets to retreat. "Seriously, Em!" I say in a sleepy, irritated voice. "You can wait! Mom and Dad aren't even up!" Rolling on my back, I hear my mother in the kitchen, starting coffee, and my father turning on the sound system in the living room.

Our family has a tradition of opening presents with Christmas music playing in the background, giving a soundtrack to our frantic shredding of paper. Nothing says Christmas to the Shelton's like Bing Crosby's White Christmas being drowned out by an over enthusiastic girl screaming, because she now owns all of the CDs of the Backstreet Boys.

With the last present opened, the cleanup project begins. Like the years before, our overjoyed thrill of opening presents always ended with my father handing me a black trash bag. Pointing from his recliner, he directs where I missed the shreds of silver glittery paper and bows, and promptly throws them in the black bag to be forgotten. "It's all fun and games until you gotta clean it up huh, son?" My father says while switching the sound system off and turning the TV to The Christmas Story. Another Shelton Family tradition - watch Christmas movies all morning until we leave for my grandmother's. With all this going on around me, I can't help but long for the isolation of the mountains with "The Guys" and being away from my family.

After the hustle of the morning, we load the minivan and head to my grandmother's for breakfast, like every year before. My grandmother was an awesome woman, living for these Christmas family breakfasts. There wasn't much gift giving, besides those intended for her but we always made sure the younger ones in the family had something to unwrap. Being sixteen, I knew I was done unwrapping gifts, so my excitement of the morning had faded to family obligations and appearances.

Standing around her kitchen table, all of our family crammed in the small room, ready to start shoveling our faces with butter drenched biscuits, greasy bacon and gravy meant for everything. Before the buffet could start, my grandmother said to my Uncle David, in her sweet southern voice, "Hey Davie, darlin'? Would you mind sayin' the blessin' before Tommy starts gnawing off his arm?" Looking at Tommy, my younger cousin, a fluffy, black haired, husky kid, who's eyes were mesmerized by the heaping mound of Cinnamon Buns at the edge of the table.

"Of course, Mama! It would be my honor!" Uncle David says, as he instructs us all to bow our heads. "Dear heavenly father, We thank you for this bounty that lies before us. We are thankful for the hands that prepared it, and most importantly, we are thankful for the best Christmas gift of all - your son." Uncle David continues as Tommy's stomach lets out a loud rumble. Holding back laughter, I keep my eyes closed, waiting for the chance to grab some food and get to the back porch, away from the mad dash of Styrofoam plates and second and third helpings. He continues, "I ask that you bless this food for the nourishment of our bodies, and keep us close in your arms. We are forever your children and thank you for all of our blessings, AMEN!" Everyone repeats his "amen" in unison, only to open our eyes to see Tommy, half way through one of the corner pieces of a Cinnamon Bun.

The drive home from my grandmother's was short yet long enough for both my sister and mother to doze off. The weight of the overly buttered, salty, fattening breakfast was too much for them as their eyes drew heavy. Listening to the Elvis Christmas Album, My father looks in the rearview mirror, trying to strike up a conversation with the only person awake in the minivan. "Hey son!", snapping up, almost dozing off myself, "Yes, Sir?" I reply, while catching his eyes darting from the road to the mirror. "So, you have big plans with your little friends this week?" Saying with a snide smile, my father rarely seemed interested in anything I was doing and having him refer to my friends as my "little friends" made my face burn. I wanted to defend them and confess to my father that they were more than friends, well, at least Colby was to me; but knowing how bad of an idea that was, I refrained.

"We are planning on skiing and maybe snowboarding", I vaguely answered, hoping to not engage him anymore than I had to. "Well that sounds interesting, seeing as you haven't stepped foot on either. Let's hope you have all your bones in the same way when you get back." He says with a big laugh as we turn into our driveway. Feeling embarrassed at the constant teasing of my father, I opened the door before the minivan was completely stopped, sending a buzzing sound through the speakers. The unwanted beeping awakens my mother and sister as my father puts the minivan in park. "Wow! I must have been more tired than I thought," says my mother while flipping down the visor to check her makeup in the flip down mirror. "Yeah, darlin' it's been a long morning. You get Em, and I'll unload the car." My father directed as I opened the door to the house, making a direct path to my bedroom.

"Son!" My mother calls from the front porch, sounding a bit frustrated. With my attention halted, she looks at my sister, "Em, honey, why don't you go to your room, and take a nap, me and Van need to have a talk." Emmalee shrugs past me, eyes closed, using nothing but her memory to guide her to her bedroom. "Son, come have a seat on the couch," my mother says, plopping herself on the opposite cushion, patting where she wanted me to sit. Sweat begins to bead from my forehead, while an inventory of my recent actions plays in my mind. I know I couldn't have possibly done anything to warrant this conversation, especially on Christmas of all days.

"Van, I know you don't have the best of luck with your father but you have to know, he comes from a good place." My mother says, in a much lower voice, more soothing than most heart-to-hearts I've had in this room. Sliding to be beside me, she wraps her arm around me and pulls me into her chest, as she continues, "Baby, he's a hard man I know, that's one thing he got from his father." Looking up on the mantle to the large, overweight, black hair man, staring down at us from the gold gilded frame. I never met my grandfather, he died right before I was born, and the holidays always made my dad crabby. Maybe that's why he forced us to listen and watch everything Christmas. Not to get us in the Christmas spirit, but to put him in the Christmas Spirit? I thought.

"Mom! You have no idea what it's like," feeling like I was on the verge of tears, I lean into my mothers cardigan sweater, "He doesn't seem to like me! I mean, I know he loves me, because he's my dad. But I can't seem to ever get anything from him but constant snide comments and making fun of me." My mother's grip gets tighter around my shoulder as she reassures me, "Honey, stop! You know your father loves you and his kidding ain't nothing but his way of saying, I love you. And anyway, you know you're smart and funny. And you even surprised us this year. You made him really proud."

Sitting up from her coddling, I look squarely at her, asking "When?" Adjusting her sweater from the creases made by my face, she looks up to give me a serious smile, "Well, for starters, at Heritage Baptist. You jumped right into the Youth Services, made friends and even played soccer." A frustrated huff escapes my chest, doubting my father would think the same as her. "I bet he didn't think I deserved the MVP award, did he?" I questioned my mother. Standing so I knew she meant business, she placed a hand on either side of my face. She leaned in, inches from my nose, concentrating her voice, clearly getting frustrated. "Now you listen, and you listen good. Your father isn't looking for every little thing that's wrong. He's proud of you. He does a lot for you and your sister and doesn't ask for much in return. I can't promise you he will ever change, but I can promise you one thing."

Looking eye to eye with my mother, I roll my eyes while asking, "What" suddenly remembering my mother hates it when anyone rolls their eyes. "Boy, if you know what's good for you, you'll roll those eyes back around and look at me." Demandingly, she continues, "The one thing you can count on, is that we will always be here to love you no matter what. You will always make us proud." And with that, she released her grip on my face, as my father barged through the front door. Holding all of the half full Tupperware containers, each balancing perfectly on top of one another, ensuring only one trip from the car to the house.

Knowing that it was a lost cause to plead my case and change my father, I grab a soda from the fridge and head to my bedroom. Shutting the door, her words replay in my head as I lean against the back of my door, frozen at what she said. "We will always be here to love you, no matter what." I wonder if she would still say that if she knew her son was going against God? Scared at the thought of God hearing my thoughts, I move to my bed, close my eyes and prepare to have a heart-to-heart with the big man upstairs.

It had been months since I actually prayed. I was feeling distant from the man who would judge me for feeling attracted to my friends, but I felt a need to get some peace before I let the day continue. With my fingers laced together, I started in my head, talking to God, "Dear heavenly father, I know it's been a while since we've spoken but I want to thank you for my family and for all you have done for us. I know that I usually come to you asking for help on a test or hoping to not get into trouble, and sometimes, even asking forgiveness for something I've done. But, today, I ask for understanding. How can the love that comes so natural to me be bad? Is it meant to keep me from you? Why do I still feel the need to be close to you? Dear Lord, I didn't ask or want these feelings. I know what I did was a sin, but I'm asking for help in understanding why I'm this way, and how you could make me in your image but allow these desires to grow every day. I'm not challenging you, Lord, but just asking for direction because my faith in you isn't getting tested, but my faith in the church is."

With that searing revelation, I close my prayer, with the usual tagline, "And father I thank you for all our blessings and ask that you watch over me and my family as we work to serve you more, AMEN!"

I felt a weight lift off my shoulders at that moment. I didn't think I could ever put into words my conflict between God and the church. During my prayer, my eyes were opened to see that the church and God were two separate things. I can love God, and still be who I am. Even if the church disagreed, I knew that God didn't hold these same prejudices. I got the feeling that God hadn't stopped listening but was allowing me the space to grow. I realized that my value was with him and not the four walls of a building or the people in it. I felt renewed on my given path as I started to pack my suitcase for the week-long snowy adventure.

Chapter Eighteen

What was expected of you is indoctrinated into every Southern Baptist from day one. When you come into this world, still clinging to your mother's breast; your training starts. You are signed up at the earliest possible age for the Children's Church, forced to memorize the Ten Commandments, and many other passages from the Bible. You are given a Sunday school teacher, a person who would kindly guide you into the fold, teaching you to understand what is a sin and what isn't.

Once you reach twelve years old, you are sent from the Children's Church to the Youth Services, where the lessons become more focused. You are drilled with sermons on purity, chastity, and abstinence. You are told your body is a temple, and needs to be respected and only you and God hold it's key. You are required to participate in vacation bible school, plays, outings, and prayer meetings. They are grooming the next generation of believers to carry out God's word, carrying on the obligations that were passed on by previous generations.

It seemed to me that a lot of the requirements of the church didn't seem necessary to me. I didn't see the need to yell out in the middle of a service, "AMEN!" or "Hallelujah!" I didn't see where I needed to only pray in the confines of a megachurch, whose membership was almost the same as the number of residents in the small town. I didn't need the stucco building to spend time with God. God was in me. And he would still direct me each day, keeping a direct line of contact, anytime I wanted it. These unnecessary obligations had to stop, and not just with the church, but my family.

Winding the mountainous roads with snow starting to appear, The Thomas' large SUV got everyone safely to the top of Sugar Mountain with ease. On our drive, I had conversations with God. Mostly when everyone was settled in with their headphones and MP3 players, or dozing off between bathroom breaks. It allowed me to find peace at who I was slowly realizing I was. I was a sixteen year old, southern gay guy, in love with his best friend.

Colby warned us that it was a long drive, but boy, was he under-selling it. A trip that would normally take an hour and a half, stretched three hours because of traffic and snow. Everyone was still exhausted from the previous day's food and festivities, many of their new presents littered the packed SUV. Half way through the drive, everyone seemed to relax into their seats, and stopped talking about what the plans were for the week.

In the very back of the SUV, the small row was left for Colby, myself, and Jeremiah. Colby's sister and her friend in the second, and of course, Coach and Ms. Patty at the front. Braydon wanted to skip this year, apparently his girlfriend's family had a tradition that Coach Thomas wasn't excited about, but allowed, seeing as though it would be a tight ride to the house. "Man, these roads make me so nauseated", Colby says, looking pale out the window. Sitting up from her co-pilot's seat, Ms. Patty turns to check on Colby. "Baby, are you going to get sick? Do you need to lay down?"

"Lay down?" I thought, where could he possibly lay down in this packed SUV. "Yeah, I think I need to, mom, but maybe it will pass." Trying to seem brave to his mother, Colby now looks green from the motion sickness. "Jeremiah, climb up with the girls, and give him some room if you don't mind," Ms. Patty says, pulling a fuzzy blanket from the open seat behind Coach Thomas. Without hesitation and in a flash, Jeremiah was buckling in the seatbelt, leaving me and Colby in the back seat.

"Hey Col, Just lay down here and it should pass soon," I say, concerned that I couldn't take away his pain. Sliding to the opposite end of the backseat, I give Colby plenty of room to lay down, thinking I would have to be cramped against the window by his feet, only to be proven wrong. Colby slides to the center seat, grabs the red sweater I had brought of his, drapes it over my lap, and lays down.

In fear, I look up to Ms. Patty, worried that she would see him choosing my lap, but only to see her resolved in him being ok, returning to her front-facing position at the front. "Oh my GOD!" I thought while surveying my situation. Colby was in my lap in the crowded car, and no one seemed to see anything wrong with that. I doubt his mother thought it was anything more than her son trying to not get sick, but to me, it was my love wanting me to help him feel better. Seeing him there in my lap, concentrating on his breathing, trying everything he could to keep from getting sick, I felt a new desire; a desire to comfort.

Lifting my hand, I slowly brush the hair from his forehead, and rub his head. My soft touch causes an instant approval from Colby, as his body relaxes and a smile creeps across his pale face. "Are you ok, Col?" I whisper, unsure if he's trying to sleep or not. "Yeah, I am, thank you for this." A tired whisper escapes Colby's tight lips. "Playing with my hair always helps relax me and makes me feel better." Nuzzling into my petting, Colby drifts off to sleep, as I rub his head and neck, selfishly making the previously boring ride peaceful.

Rounding the final curve of the mountain, our ears all popped from the elevation change, rows of stately homes appear in the treetops. "Almost there you guys!" Says Coach Thomas in a concentrated tone, trying to make sure to keep the SUV on the road and not in a snowbank. "Once we get there, we unload the SUV and we get settled in for the night." His voice wakes Colby as he rolls on his back, still nestled in my lap. Stretching and opening his eyes, me and Colby smile at one another as I notice the return of his loving twinkle in his eyes.

"How was the nap?" I ask, worried, that he would still feel motion sickness. "I needed that nap! I feel much better!" Colby says, turning his head in my stomach, wrapping his arms around my buckled waist, gripping to give me a hug. "Thank you, Van, I knew you would make me feel better." He says, sitting up, rubbing the sleep from his eyes. "You feel better honey?" Noticing her son appearing in the backseat, Ms. Patty turns to get a better look at how Colby looked. "Ah, the color is back, I think you're back to normal!" She says, flashing him a smile. "You better thank Van, because you've been crowding that poor boy in the seat for seventy-five miles." Giggling at her own joke, she turns back around as Colby's hand reaches for mine. Enlacing his fingers in mine behind the seat, he looks up at me and whispers, "You have no idea how thankful I am."

"We're here." Coach Thomas announces, as he turns to pull into a log cabin house, situated at the top of the Sugar Mountain Range. Pulling into the driveway, everyone sits up to survey the area and gawk at all the freshly laid snow. "This never gets old." Coach Thomas says, looking over at Ms. Patty as he parks next to the backdoor. The house was huge. Balconies on every door and window, allowing every room to have a private view of the mountain range. The dark logs of the exterior give a stark contrast to the pristine white snow covering everything in sight. Sitting up to look around, I could see a chair lift in the far distance behind the house, looking as though it was miles away.

"If you look up there kids, that's where we will be skiing tomorrow." Ms. Pat says, pointing out the windshield at the top of the mountain. "We will be up there tomorrow, almost touching the heavens. Even though I won't be skiing, I'll be up there with you guys, holding all of your things when you get to the bottom of the slopes." Wasting no time, Colby and his father jump out of the SUV and grab the snow shovels by the porch and make a path to the door. "You kids, wait here while we get the area cleared and then we can unload."

Jeremiah looks back at me from the middle seat, removing the headphones that had been in his ears since we left, "Man, this is going to be great!" He says, putting his sweater and jacket on. "I've been skiing in Colorado with my cousins, but that was way more crazy than I think this place will be." Trying to sound confident, but instead seeming arrogant. "I've never skied so this should be interesting," with a nervous tone to my voice, "I'm scared to break something, but I won't know until I try it." Finding the courage to accept my fate; I was going to do this, and I was going to do everything I could to remember this trip for the rest of my life.

Chapter Nineteen

Courage isn't something that you train for, it's something that you have to find in the moment. It is needed to get through a difficult time and sometimes, it allows you to start something that will change the path of the rest of your life. Courage is found when you step out of fear, and charge head first into life. You may not know the exact place you'll end up, but courage pushes you along the paths as you navigate the turns in your life.

Over the last year, I found my courage. My courage wasn't in the walls of a church or in the halls of a school. It was found within me, inside my heart and mind. I had the courage to allow my erratic emotions and feelings to grow and allowed them to take me to unknown places. And even with my confused desires, I found the courage to try something new.

I found the strength to persevere through fear, insecurities, and wanting to be accepted. I had the courage to tell myself that I was actually gay, and that I belonged. Though I hadn't found the courage to make it public, I knew at some point in my life, I would have the fearlessness to make that declaration. But until then, I was happy with who I had become. I was finally happy in my own skin.

Grabbing an ice pack from the freezer, Ms. Patty walked over to the leather oversized couches in the main living room. "Here honey, put this on your ankle to keep the swelling down." Handing me the frozen blue brick as she told me, "I'll call your mom and let her know that you are ok, and you'll have a great skiing story to tell her."

"Van! I swear, I didn't see you! I'm so sorry!" Jeremiah apologizes. "I feel so bad! I promise I couldn't stop!" Jeremiah continues apologizing as I wrap a towel around my swollen foot.

"Jer, It's ok man!" I reassure him. "I had fallen like fifty times before you came down the slope. There's no way you could have seen me." Placing the subzero pack on my sore ankle sent a searing cold up my body, yet it was strangely providing some relief. "I barely had gotten up and balanced when you came around the turn. And nothing is broken, honestly, I took a harder hit from Braydon on the soccer field than from you." Adding insult to his apology, I flash a smirk at him, making him look up at me. "Oh now wait a minute! There is no way Braydon hit you harder, because I was flying down the slopes, carving out lines all the way down." Jeremiah sits up, trying to save what self esteem he had left after plowing down his friend.

"Man! You act like you were in the Olympics going for the gold!" Colby says in jest. "It wasn't even the level 2 slope; it was the bunny slope!" Slapping Jeremiah, Colby burst out laughing, causing a smile to force its way across Jeremiah's face. "We had to get warmed up, you know!" Jeremiah is still trying to seem like the pro in the group. "Yeah! Warmed up with a snow ski right into the back of my head!" I say rubbing the knot now popping up on the back of my head. "I wouldn't be surprised if I had a black eye tomorrow. If I do end up with a black eye, you're telling my mother!" I say, knowing the dramatics and questions she would have.

"I really am sorry man!" With one last apology, Jeremiah walks to the

Repentance of the Southern Burden | 127

kitchen where Ms. Pat was pouring hot cocoa into mugs for everyone. Alone in the living room, Colby leans in so only I can hear him. "Van, are you sure you're ok?" A worried tone in his voice. Leaning over to remove the ice brick from my now numb ankle to assess the injury, "Yes, I promise! I'm fine. See!" Pointing at my ankle, smaller than it was five minutes earlier. "The swelling is going down, and I can move my toes. Nothing is broken and I'm sure I'll be ok by tomorrow to get back on the skis."

Resolved in my answer, Colby looks into the kitchen to see everyone chatting at the bar, looking at brochures for the tubing excursion we were going on tomorrow. Leaning in again, this time to steal a quick kiss. Shocked at his brazen action, less than five feet from everyone, I look at him like a deer in headlights. "Col, you are crazy! What if they see?" I whisper, in disbelief. "I don't care", Colby says, as he lifts his hand to brush the hair from my eyes. "I've been wanting to do that all day, especially after seeing you get mowed down by Jeremiah." His voice seemed to tremble while his eyes looked down at my exposed foot. "I don't know how to explain it Van, but seeing you in pain, all I wanted to do was to pick you up, and rescue you."

Laying back on the couch, not caring about the others nearby, I grab his hand from my face, pulling it to my chest. "Colby, you have no idea how many times I have had that dream. A dream of being swept off my feet." Looking back at the group of people in the kitchen, they were oblivious to our Lifetime movie moment. "I just had no idea that getting swept off my feet meant getting pummeled into the snow by Jeremiah and being thrown over your father's shoulder. And on the bunny slope! There were toddlers soaring past us as he carried me to the side." Letting go of my hand, Colby burst into laughter. "I wasn't going to say anything, but yes, kids were everywhere and yes, they all saw it happen."

Our laughter got the attention of everyone in the kitchen as Coach

Thomas brought mugs of cocoa to me and Colby. "How's our patient doing?" He says, placing the mugs on the knotty pine oversized coffee table in front of where we were sitting. "Oh, I think he's going to be fine, but he may need an amputation." Colby says, slapping my shoulder and laughing. "You ain't cutting nothing off of me!" I protest, knowing he's joking. "Even if you were a doctor, and on the off chance that I actually did need to have it cut off, you ain't coming near me with no type of saw."

Coach Thomas pats Colby on the shoulder and chuckles at the friendly banter between me and Colby. "Well, we are planning on going tubing down the south side of the mountain tomorrow. If your foot still hurts, I don't want you going down those slopes. You can just hang out with Patty in the lodge." Coach Thomas says, taking the blue ice pack from the coffee table, and placing it back on my ankle. Trying to put his mind at ease, I stand up, showing that I can bear weight on my own. "I promise Coach, I'll be ok. I think I just bruised it." Showing my ability to stand, I grab the ice pack in one hand, and use Colby's shoulder to stand up. The weight of my body on my sprained ankle sends sparks of pain through my body. Knowing I had to fake it and act like nothing hurt, so I wouldn't miss out on the fun of tomorrow's tubing excursion.

Presuming I was ok, Coach Thomas agreed to wait until morning for my final decision on going down the slopes again. "You boys ready to play some cards?" Ms. Patty says rounding the side of the opposite couch. "I'm ready to kick some butt in Phase 10!" She says, grabbing a stack of cards out of the table beside the river-stoned fireplace. "Heck yeah! I'm game!" I say, while hobbling over to the kitchen table. "Mom, me and Destiny are going to go hang out in our room, is that ok?" Colby's sister asks, bored at the thought of playing a game with her family and her brother's friends. "That's fine baby, just don't stay up too late, I'll wake you girls up for breakfast, and remember to keep the music down when me and your father go to bed." Assuring her mother, the girls run down the hallway to the room, slamming the door, keeping themselves entertained away from everyone else.

"You boys can be as loud as you want, but those girls are right next to our room." Coach Thomas says with a laugh. "I don't think I can handle another night of hearing Macy giggling and Destiny talking all night." Rolling his eyes to meet Ms. Patty perturbed expression. "You know it's annoying to you too." Looking at his wife for validation. "Honey, it's a vacation, and yes, they are loud at our house, but we don't hear them down the hall." Ms. Patty says, dividing the cards and starting to shuffle.

Pulling a chair out, Coach sits at the table with Jeremiah, Colby, myself and Ms. Patty. Leaning in to whisper, making sure that his voice wasn't heard by his daughter down the hall, "Now, you boys." His voice trailing off, as he takes a final look down the hallway, "You boys can be as loud as you want. We can't hear a thing down there, so you guys enjoy that game room." His favoritism for his son was apparent with his ensuring we had the basement game room to ourselves. "You guys can play pool or air hockey all night, and we won't care!" At the words, all night, Ms. Patty stops shuffling, "Jerry! Don't you dare give these boys permission to stay up all hours of the night!" Her words were accented by her pounding the decks to smooth the loose cards for another shuffle. "I'm not dealing with a house full of sleepy teenagers tomorrow."

Giving his wife a mischievous smile, he promises to make sure we know to get at least a few hours of rest before morning. All three of us agree, as the cards are dealt and the card game begins. "Now, you boys know how sweet my wife is?" Asks Coach Thomas, gathering his cards and placing them in their hopeful position in his hand. "She's all sweet and nice, until cards are involved." He says, jokingly giving his wife a snarl. "She's the undertaker!" Colby interjects. "She does care if you are a friend or even her own flesh and blood!" He says, leaning into his father, matching his gaze at Ms. Patty. "You guys better hush! You're making me out like I do it on purpose!" Colby's mother says, holding back a laugh. "It's how the cards are dealt! I can't help you suck at cards and that I'm so darn good at them." The table erupted into laughter as the game started with Ms. Patty laying her full phase down, getting the one card she needed to complete her phase with her first draw. "See! Told ya!" Coach says, peering over his cards at Ms. Patty, frustrated at his wife's card shark abilities.

All of the joking and laughing sent me into another place. My family played cards a lot. Usually with my father's family but rarely allowing the kids to join the adults. Sitting at the table with my friend's parents was a new experience for me, one that I could see myself getting used to. The tone of everyone's joking wasn't mean spirited. No one was really made fun of, it was all part of the fun - everyone's fun. And everyone knew that we were only kidding, a stark difference to my family. Had some of the jokes been thrown at the table with my family, the game would have ended because someone refused to continue because their feelings were hurt. It only took me a few phases to start joining in on the poking fun, and it made me feel like I was part of the family. The new experience was only topped by the occasional tap on my uninjured foot under the table. Undoubtedly, from Colby, showing his inability to hide affection for me. Each tap and rub sent pulses up my leg and into my crotch. I knew then that the new experiences of the evening wouldn't be only involving cards, but would be reserved for a party of two - me and Colby.

Chapter Twenty

Growth can happen in full sight of those around you. Like a fully bloomed flower, the stem and petals are a mere product of months of underground growth and watering. Giving strong roots to support the prize that was above the surface for the world to see and enjoy. I had grown during these discovery times. The processes most unseen by anyone but by me and by God. I found a sense of belonging and pride in my own path. I knew I could be the trailblazer and break the obligations placed on me. Repentance wasn't needed because of who I was. It wasn't something that needed forgiveness; who I was just needed to be found and nurtured.

Before finding out who I was, the thought of being confident in my own skin was foreign and unobtainable. In my discovery, I had finally been able to grow into my new self and started accepting that I was who I was; and no one could change me. I was still loved by God for who I was and I wouldn't be made to feel otherwise. Growth in God is personal, and can't be mapped out for you by someone else. I held the pen to the map of my life, and I was happy to finally have the strength to take control of my own adventures.

An adventure can open itself to expose something that needed closure, giving you the ability to move past something that was holding you back. But moving past it doesn't mean you forget it. It just means you have grown because of it. Using it as a stepping stone to get to where you are now, happy and grateful for the encounter.

Coach Thomas was right, Ms. Patty was brutal at playing cards. She finished out her final Phase with the rest of us barely able to pass Phase 6. Accomplished in her goal of winning, she stands from the table, leaving her winning hand on the table as a monument of her success. "I'm heading to bed boys, Jerry you comin' to bed?" She asks, looking at Coach Thomas as he releases a full body yawn. "Yep! Right behind you!" Standing from the table, looking as Ms. Patty walks down the hallway, he leans into "The Guys." "You boys hang out tonight, have fun. I'll keep the Misses off your back in the morning." Putting a finger over his lips, he reminds us to keep it a secret and shhhh, worried that our laughter would expose his permission for us to misbehave.

Grabbing some snacks from the counter and a few sodas out of the fridge, we head down the two flights of stairs to the game room for some true "Guy" time. Settling in the recliner, Jeremiah flips the TV on as me and Colby set up the snacks on the coffee table. "Who's sleeping on the couch?" Jeremiah says, pointing out that there were only two bedrooms off the game room. Unsure of what he wanted, I looked up from the snacks and asked him where he would prefer to sleep. "Well, in a bed of course!" Choosing a bedroom, left me or Colby with the couch. But I didn't take into account the unknown third option.

"Ok, that works for me." Colby says, walking over to me, grabbing me around my waist. "Van can sleep in my room, no need for anyone to be on this lumpy thing." Giving me a stronger tug, pulling me into his body, I could tell this was his plan all along. "You ok with that?" He asks, looking over at me, with eyes begging for a yes. "Let me think about this for a second," trying to sound not-so excited at the prospect of Colby and I having a room to ourselves, alone. "A lumpy couch or a king sized bed? I'll take the bed over that any day."

Unaroused by our playful jest, Jeremiah flips through channels on the tv, searching for something to peak his interest. "Whatever you guys want, it doesn't matter to me." He says, unfazed. "I'm probably going to be heading to bed soon anyways, I'm more tired than I thought." Jeremiah says, chugging the last of his Dr. Pepper down in one gulp. "Yeah, I'm really tired too," Colby says, lifting his brow, signaling my acknowledgment of advances. Seeing what he was saying, I thought of a quick excuse that would allow me to head to the bedroom too.

"I think I'm going to go lay down now because my foot is killing me." I say, acting like my foot was unable to hold my weight. At the word of my injured foot, Jeremiah sits up from the recliner, and gives me another apologetic grimace. "Dude, I'm really sorry about today. I feel so bad." Ashamed at making him feel bad, I tried to reassure him that I was ok, but just needed to get off my feet to allow the swelling to stay down. Assured of my acting, Jeremiah returns to the TV, watching ESPN Sports Recap. Turning to head to the bedroom, Colby reaches his hand out, sliding his palm across the small of my back as I walk past him.

"Yeah, I'm heading to bed, man. I'll catch you in the morning." Engrossed in the sportscaster's commentary on best touchdowns throughout history, Jeremiah gives an uncaring, "Night," as Colby follows me to the bedroom - our bedroom. Flipping the light on in the room, the stark white duvet is brightly displayed on a dark walnut four poster bed. The room was tastefully decorated with a mountain lodge theme, fitting for the ski retreat. Looking around at the room, I see pictures of the Thomas family scattered around the room in various decorative frames. Leaning in to get a better look, I can see Colby as a small child, in white and turquoise ski gear. His father stood over him smiling, holding him up on the very slope that I was run over by Jeremiah.

"That was my seventh birthday." Colby says, shutting the door behind him as he walks in. "My parents brought me up here that year and the family all stayed in the house." Colby's voice is soft and sweet, as he remembers how happy he was to have everyone together for him. "Every aunt, uncle and cousin was here. We had air beds everywhere!" He laughs at the memory of stepping over sleeping bodies just to get to the bathroom in the middle of the night. He continues, "this place has always been a place of happiness for me. I've always felt alive here and able to breathe."

Lavishing his story, I sit on the end of the bed, as my heart begins to yearn for a place like that in his mind. I wanted to fill a small corner of his heart the way those memories had. Before I could ask more about that ski trip, Colby reaches down to stand me up from the bed. "I've been waiting all day," correcting himself, "well, actually two weeks for this, and I want to take my time." My heart melted in his arms.

Leaning in to me, our lips met with a spark shooting from our lips, igniting a flame of passion that had been held prisoner to our social obligations. His arms wrapped around my waist, pulling me closer into his embrace as his mouth trailed from my lips to my cheek. Taking a hand under my chin, he tips my head back, exposing my neck to his wanting. Kissing a trail over to my ear lobe, he continues down my neck, settling on my collar bone. Chills rush my body as new areas of my body are explored by way of his mouth. We couldn't hold back any longer and we needed this, we wanted this, and we had every intention of experiencing it together.

Pushing me to sit on the bed, unwilling to release the touch of his mouth to my body, he pulls my shirt over my head as I say "I don't know what to do, but I'm willing to try anything." My words shaking in anticipation. "I don't know either, but I do know, I want this.

***

*I want to taste you, and feel you in any way I can." His words determined and exact. Throwing his shirt off, he returns his lips to my neck, causing my body to cover with goosebumps. His hands lightly caressing every inch of my awakened body, now fiery with his attention.

Moving his mouth to between my pecs, he places his hand on my shoulder, affirming that he was in charge and in this moment, he was there to pleasure me. I subdue, allowing my body to relax, eyes closed, as my fears run away and my dreams come true. Reaching my nipples, he drops small kisses at the pitched skin, followed by his tongue circling around until bringing them into his lips. Giving each a subtle sucking, making them erect. The bliss provided to me caused a loud moan to escape my lungs. Scared to be heard, but remembered what Coach said to us when we left for bed, "We can't hear anything down there." And not caring if Jeremiah heard us, I grant myself the moment of sheer abandonment of silence.

His kisses continued down my stomach, to my navel then to my hips. The connection of kisses and tongue actions sent pleasure in a way I didn't know was possible. The kisses on my hips caused my body to thrust upwards, increasing his eagerness and attention. By the time his hands were on the waist of my shorts, I was begging for him to keep going. "Yes, don't stop!" I begged, barely able to form words as my heart continued racing. Running his thumb under my waistband, he traces around my body, lifting my butt off the bed. Seizing the moment, he grabs a handful of the fabric and slowly pulls them down.

My cock springs out, slapping my stomach with a loud smack. "Damn!" he exclaims. Bypassing my aching cock, his kisses around to my thighs, now burning with desire. Embracing my thighs in his arms, enlaced around my body, he slides me down the bed, my legs hanging off the bed. Kneeling between my legs, he pushes my thighs wider to grant him access to all of my manhood. Sitting back on his heels, I look down and see him smiling up at me. "You really are beautiful Donovan. When I've pictured this happening in my head, I could never have imagined you being more perfect." My cheeks blush as I sit up, grabbing him under his arms, pulling him to lay on top of me. "I want this, and I want you." Reassuring him, I reach down and pull his pants off, throwing them across the room.

Feeling his body pressed against mine almost sent me over the edge. Bearing his hips into mine as his lips connect to my mouth, I feel his cock jump from the electric pulses created by our bodies. Realizing where this was heading, I sat up, unsure of being ready to either receive him in me or vice versa. "I don't know if I can have you, you know, in me." Sounding scared at the thought of him being inside me, though I wanted everything, I knew my body would have limitations. We both were inexperienced and neither was prepared for that step. "I hadn't planned on that" unfazed by my fear, Colby slides his hands between us and grabs onto my dick. "But what I had planned on, was having this in my mouth until I tasted it down my throat."

His words send my head spinning as I lean back down on the bed, giving him full access to use me for his exploration. Wasting no time, he positioned himself back between my legs, taking his hands to rub the inside of my thighs. Without hesitation, he props my cock up with one hand, and licks the length of my shaft. The warmth of his mouth caused my cock to jump erratically. The first time pleasure was invigorating and I had to have more. Taking my hand, I placed it on the back of his neck, showing that I needed more. He takes my cock between his lips and allows the head to pass through to his tongue.

In my head, words were coming out of my mouth, but in the ambiance of the room, only a faint whimper was heard. Finding his gag reflex, Colby settles into a comfortable depth, and picks up speed. Feeling his hand at the base of my cock, squeezing as he bobs up and down my head, allowing more and more of it to pass down his throat. Knowing I was reaching orgasm, I pulled him off me; not ready for this to end.

"I want to try something" I say, turning my body so my head was now on the edge of the bed. "Lay on your side, and we can both taste each other." Surprised by my own dominance, I slide to center my body on my beloved. Greedy at the prospect of a new feeling, I reach around his waist, pulling his leaking cock into my mouth. His extreme girth becomes apparent as my jaw stretches to allow his shaft to pass along my lips. Realizing what I was wanting to do, Colby reaches around my waist and pulls my cock into his mouth. Feeling his mouth around my manhood caused my balls to tighten, knowing I was close, I pulled off of him, giving him a warning.

Steadfast, he pushes further down on my cock, reiterating his desire to taste me. Wanting the same from him, I take his meat back into my mouth. In the next thrust, I empty into his mouth as his cock swells, erupting spurts of warm liquid, one after another into my mouth. Unable to keep it all, some spills out of the side of my mouth as I release more and more into his. Slowing his pace, lavishing the taste, he changes his attention to the head of my dick, wasting none of my jizz on the bed, he swallows every ounce.

Releasing his cock from my mouth, I swallow thickly, pushing the salty liquid to my stomach. A warm sensation fills my body, as my need for Colby intensifies. My mind was willing but my body was spent. Spinning around in the bed, allowing my lover and I to be face to face, Colby kisses my lips. A salty taste, different from that in my mouth, lingered on his lips, as we explored the scents and tastes of each other on our bodies. "That was…" Colby's words unable to find him. "Van, that was beyond amazing, and well worth the wait." Unable to pull away from his embrace, I lose myself in his lips, allowing our kiss to continue until both of our cocks go soft between us. **

***

"I don't know what to think." I say, pulling the covers out from under us, pushing my feet through the sheets. "I have never felt more alive than I do right now." Leaning into my lover's shoulders. "I told you" Colby says while giving me a peck on my temple. "I know this is all new, but I'm willing to see what happens day by day." He says, pushing his arm under my neck, as I nuzzle into his body. "So, does this mean we are… you know?" I ask, unsure of what to call us. It seemed childish to say boyfriend, but honestly, I didn't know what two guys who felt what we did for one another, called it.

"Well, I don't like labels. I've never had what you would call a girlfriend. I've had girls I've liked but never put a label on it." Colby says, yawning from the adrenaline that was crashing post orgasm. "I don't need a label, but I'm ok with saying I'm gay. But I'm not wanting to tell anyone yet. Are you ok with that?" I ask, nervous that my question was too intense for the moment. "I don't know what I am Van, but I know where I want to be, and who I want to be with." Feeling happy with who we were to each other, I allow my body to relax. Still naked under the cool cotton sheets, I close my eyes and start to feel the need to pray. Unable to shake the feelings; I give in.

"Dear Lord" I think to myself, "I'm sure you saw all of that happen, and I know what the Bible says and what we have learned in church. I just wanted you to know that whatever happened between Colby and I, that I'm thankful for it. A year ago, I didn't have a place or a purpose. But today, I'm in the arms of someone who cherishes me. Someone that I know will walk alongside me, and wants me to be a better me." I continue thinking as Colby shifts his body to fall fast asleep.

"Your word is filled with countless analogies for the word love, many of which I don't understand. But what I can understand is what I feel for Colby. I'm not prepared to tell him yet or say it, but I know you will understand when I tell you. I do love him. I'm connected to him. I feel you placed him in my path to teach me, hold me, and protect me from the pain of Jeremiah. You knew I would need someone to love me for who I was and make me realize that I was ok. I know I will never understand why you chose for me to have the encounter with Jeremiah first, but in your infinite wisdom, you did. Jeremiah may not have wanted things to happen the way they did, but I for one am grateful. I want to thank you dear Jesus. Not for the experiences, but for giving me the ability to see love around me. I don't feel that me being gay is a curse; I see it as a blessing. Thank you for giving me this life, and I will forever be grateful for the future you have planned for me. Please continue to watch over my family, and continue to bless all of us in all of our endeavors. Please watch over us as we grow to be closer in your loving arms. Amen!"

Epilogue

Figuring out that my relationship with God wasn't based solely on my presence in a man made building, sitting in the pews with other church-goers. My connection to God was between him and I, and that could be anywhere. Though I still went to church and kept active, my relationship with God grew based on my personal growth and not what was forced upon me. I got a job, started to save for a car, and even though I worked a lot, I still tried to make it too as many of the church activities on the weekends I could attend. Yet each Sunday, I made sure to be sitting next to Colby in a pink pew. After realizing that Colby felt the same as I did, we tried to spend as much time as we could together. Our jobs and school were demanding but thankfully for me, but thankfully for me, Colby worked across town, allowing me to focus on work after school with little distractions.

We never put a label on what we had, and I was ok with that since the ski trip. Now with summer approaching, I was eager to figure out what types of excursions and adventures we would experience together. "The Guys" group was still intact, but our lives all started to morph as we approached summer break.

"Hey Van!" My mother yells down the hall to my room, "Honey! Can you come to the kitchen? I want to show you something." Frustrated to be pulled from my first day off in two weeks. "Yes ma'am!" I say through a clenched jaw. Walking into the kitchen, I see the counter littered with Summer Camp brochures. "Honey, we've been saving up and got the money together to send you to the Camp Cardinal's Nest this summer!" The excitement beamed in her eyes. "Your father talked to the youth leaders and the parents and everyone agrees that this would be great for the Youth Group." Confusion was plastered on my face.

"My father planned this?" I ask, worried that my father would pick the cheapest, manliest place in the state that I'm sure I would hate. In protest, I begged my mother to rethink her plans, only to be reminded of how much they worked to save for the basic deposit. "Honey, you might as well just give up, because you're going!" Not wavering, I kept trying to come up with any excuse in the book to keep me from going, only to have them shot down by my mother's brilliant persistence.

"I spoke to Patty and Denise, and Colby and Jeremiah are going too." She says, cutting me off mid-complaining. "Van, I'm glad you finally gave up because your application has been sent." My mother's laughter rings down the hallway to my room. Even though I didn't want to go, I mostly didn't want to explain to my boss that I needed to take a one-week vacation for a church camp. The only positive thing was getting to spend an entire week with Colby.

Turning my computer on, the familiar, "You've Got Mail" jingle sounded through the speakers. I had given up on checking my emails since searching for a job last month. After filling out applications all over town my email inbox was full of department store spam. Looking at the Chat boxes, I see a few friends online and see Jeremiah and Colby both were online. Shooting Colby a message first, I send him a smiley face and <3. It was our secret code asking if it was ok to chat freely.

Not getting a response, I close the Instant messenger and click on Jeremiah's screen name. "I wonder if his parents have told him yet," I wondered.

SPORTZ4U2NV: Hey man! Wassup?

TREBLEMAKER16: N2M u?

SPORTZ4U2NV: N2M, just chillin. Has your parents told you the news yet?

TREBLEMAKER16: Yep, just got the bomb dropped on me five minutes ago. Thoughts?

I was curious to see what he thought about going on this trip. Waiting for his response, I started searching the internet for Camp Cardinal's Nest, only to find a basic website with kids on canoes on a huge lake, and the massive mountain lodge with a stone fireplace and stuffed deer over the mantle.

SPORTZ4U2NV: Well, I actually am looking forward to it. I think it will be fun. I'm sure we can all room together. Mom says it's like a dorm setting. Girls on one floor, and guys on the top floor.

TREBLEMAKER16: Sounds interesting. Just don't know about the hiking. Their site says they do a five mile wilderness hike, overnight in the woods.

SPORTZ4U2NV: Well, at least you still have your sleeping bag that fits two people.

I couldn't believe what I was seeing. This was the first time he ever brought up anything that happened between "The Guys." Unsure of what to reply with, I just send a basic response:

TREBLEMAKER16: I'll have to find it, it's somewhere around here.

Hopefully that will keep him off the topic, because I doubt he wants to have a full conversation about those nights.

SPORTZ4U2NV: Well, At least Colby can get the pleasure of having that experience, guess I missed my chance.

My heart began to thunder in my chest, was he actually telling me he was regretting not taking the leap? Or was he just trying to play along. I couldn't think of a response before he was replaying back.

SPORTZ4U2NV: That first night at the ski trip, I heard you guys. I know what happened, and I wished it was me. I know it may be too late, but If you ever want to, you know, do something, the woods would be open to us the entire trip.

Trying to figure out what to say to Jeremiah, and rationalize what was actually happening, my notification goes off. It was Colby. Thank God, this temptation was going to go away.

SOCCRALLSTAR: Smiley Face <3

TREBLEMAKER16: Smiley Face <3. I got the weirdest message from Jer. He heard us at the ski trip.

SOCCRALLSTAR: Ah man! Seriously? What did you say?

TREBLEMAKER16: I haven't said anything yet, but he seems like he feels like he missed his chance, and is actually talking about what happened at your house.

SOCCRALLSTAR: Well, he needs to realize that you belong in my arms and noone else's.

A perfect response from the perfect man.

SOCCRALLSTAR: You still feel the same way right?

Realizing I hadn't given him a response, I panic!

TREBLEMAKER16: Oh yes, no one's arms belong around me but yours.

Settled in my gut, I prepare my response to Jeremiah. Opening his chat window, I start my monologue of shooting him down while trying to salvage what would be left of our friendship after.

TREBLEMAKER16: Hey Jer, Don't beat yourself up! We all were just trying things out, and honestly, Col and I don't have any type of labels but I'm not doing anything with anyone else. I'm completely happy now. I want to keep our friendship awesome, and I couldn't live with myself if I lost my best friend.

SPORTZ4U2NV: I understand, but I'll try to change your mind at Camp Cardinal's Nest, you'll see.

And with that, he closes his chat, and logs off. I swear he argues like my mother, has to have the last word no matter what. But what did he mean by ``he'll change my mind?'' There's no way, my mind was set for only one guy, Colby and that wasn't going to change, but how do I close my eyes to my first love.

Overwhelmed, I sent off a Smiley Face and <3 to Colby, signaling our safe conversation had ended, and logged off of AOL. Laying in my bed, my mind begins to spin like it had a year ago. Why is it that anytime Jeremiah is involved, my brain does somersaults until my heart is in knots. I couldn't possibly walk away from a sure thing with Colby just for a chance with Jeremiah. But if I don't see this through, I'll always wonder, "What if?" Or worse, he could tell my parents of my adventures with Colby.

Either way, I had a few weeks to figure out the details. But right now, I wanted to get ready for my weekend at Colby's house. I hope his parents call it an early night, giving us free reign to just be in each other's arms. I needed him now more than ever to show me how much he wanted me, and the ability to show him how much I needed him. I never in a million years would have thought I was going to be causing a wedge between my best friend and my lover.

ABOUT THE AUTHOR

J.R. Gray-Heim (Joshua) grew up surrounded by family on their original homestead, nestled on the side of Spencer Mountain in Dallas, NC. As an older Millennial, he played a balancing act between Southern religious obligations and self-acceptance.

Once his grandmother passed away, Joshua finally came out to himself and felt the freedom to begin dating the same sex for the first time. Then he began the long journey of coming out to friends and family as he became more confident in his truth. Today Joshua lives with his husband, Adam, and three dogs in Raeford, a small suburb of Fayetteville, NC, home to Fort Bragg. As a business owner and a philanthropist, he lives by the mantra, "make a difference, not a dollar," and spends much of his free time giving back to the community in a variety of ways.

He also spends quite a bit of time antiquing and hunting for vintage treasures, much to his husband's chagrin at times. His talents span everything from performing in drag brunches to landscape painting to singing in a barbershop chorus.

Joshua's biggest desire in life is to create a sense of connection and belonging for everyone he encounters and for those who read his story. As he loves to tell folks, "You only get one life; make it count. Trust me, honey, you got this."

www.jrgrayheim.com

Lightning Source UK Ltd.
Milton Keynes UK
UKHW021052180522
403172UK00009B/972